The Shadow of Dusk

Dan Djurdjevic

Pikkeljig Press

Third edition 2024
First edition published as *A Hazy Shade of Twilight and other nightmares* 2015

Pikkeljig Press
PO Box 388
Bayswater 6933 Australia
www.pikkeljig.com

Cover photograph of Titan and Rhea by NASA
Back cover photograph of author by Peta Santoro

ISBN-13: 978-0-9876233-5-5

Temptation

I stood outside her door wondering whether to knock. It wasn't open – just ajar – and through the gap I could see her sitting at her desk, the familiar lines etched between her eyebrows, unwashed, dark hair tucked behind one ear. Her eyes seemed puffy, bruised even. I could smell her acetone breath from the doorway as she sighed. But that's how we all were. It came with the job.

I knew I was at a point of no return – but I didn't care. I was like a kid playing with radium: transfixed by its sickly glow and unable to understand the danger. So I tapped lightly and the door swung open slowly as a result (everything there seemed to float perpetually). Leila looked up from her screen, brow still furrowed.

'Edin… Hello.'

'Still at it eh?' I winced a bit as I heard the levity in my voice.

'Unfortunately,' she sighed again and leaned back in her chair rubbing her eyes. 'And I've got this blasted headache. Just background, but it never goes. I think I'm sensitive to trace amounts of hydrogen cyanide. That's just a guess. Bloody stuff somehow still gets into the air supply despite my best efforts.' She leaned forward and cupped her chin in her hands. 'And you? Had enough?'

'Yes,' I said laughing, 'that's for sure.' She didn't react, her eyes focused somewhere in the middle distance. The silence that followed was no more than a few seconds but it seemed an eternity.

'Looks like we're in for an early nightfall. Have you seen...'

'Why are you here Edin?'

I opened my mouth but it felt dry and no sound came out. Leila continued to regard me with her dark, hooded eyes, head still resting on her palms. I swallowed.

'Well... I was just going to...'

'Sometimes I think I've forgotten my own reasons. You know?'

'Sorry?'

'Well at first it was so glamorous. An adventure. A roller-coaster ride. But of course that didn't last very long. After a while it was just a new way of living. You settle into a routine. Which has its advantages. But then you wonder what the hell you're doing. Don't you agree?'

'I guess so...'

'You still haven't answered my question. What brought you here?'

'Like you said. That whole glamour thing, for sure. There was the curiosity. I suppose there was also some element of competition.'

'You men are so competitive!'

'Fair cop,' I said. Except I didn't agree in the slightest. I hadn't met anyone as competitive as Leila but it didn't seem the right time to debate stereotypes. So I breathed in, like a man who's had a narrow escape, and said: 'You mention the whole routine thing. I'm finding myself doing what I used to do back home. Long hours at work. Watching a video or two back in my room, maybe playing a computer game. Sleep. Then back to work again.'

'What's the matter – can't hack it?' Leila was still cupping her chin and I wondered whether she was serious

– then noticed a grin creasing one corner of her lips. I laughed.

'Yes – I suppose I can't! That's why I'm knocking off and you're still hard at work.'

'You act like there's something else to do.'

'Isn't there?'

'Not really. You see, I've realised why I'm here: I have a job to finish. I'm on a countdown. Soon I'll be gone and I'll forget this place ever existed. Back home, back to my friends. No offence.'

'None taken,' I said, lying.

'I'm not here to have fun. Anyway, I can't stand computer games. Waste of bloody time. What do you men see in the damned things?'

'Some women like computer games too…'

Leila snorted and leaned back with her fingers linked behind her head. I could see sweat stains under her armpits. 'This one certainly doesn't. I particularly hate the shooting ones.'

'Well, it passes the time.'

'Sleep works well enough for me,' she replied.

'Come on! Surely you have something you like to do besides sleep?'

'Does reading count?'

'How about just having a chat with a colleague?'

'That's what we're doing right now aren't we?'

'Yes, well… I mean without a screen full of work in front of one of us. You know – like when you're having a drink or something.'

Leila started to laugh. A full belly laugh. She leaned back so far in her chair I wondered whether she might fall over. 'Edin, you're not asking me out are you?'

'Don't be silly.' I could feel my face reddening.

'You act like you're a single man. What would your wife

say?'

'Suggesting a drink with a colleague is hardly asking someone out, especially in this God-forsaken place.'

Leila continued to chuckle and wiped tears from the sides of her eyes. 'You crack me up, you know that?'

I had started to back out. 'Have it your way. Just thought you could use a bit of a break.'

'Why?' Her laughter had stopped.

'Why what?' I paused in the doorway.

'Break? What the hell point is there?'

'The point is… that's what we humans do. You seem to have forgotten.' I walked towards her screen and pointed. 'This stuff… work. It isn't everything. There are other things in life.'

'This isn't life.'

'What is it then? A bad dream?'

'It's something we just have to do.'

'Until what? You go home in a year? What happens if you don't even live that long? I mean, have you even looked outside today? Have you seen the sun in this cycle?'

'No, I probably haven't. I don't get windows – as you can see.' Leila waved her arm around the four walls.

'Well nightfall is coming. Early – because winter is setting in. We're about to start maybe twelve straight days of darkness. And you don't even seem to care.'

'Why should I?'

'You know perfectly well! Or at least, you should. Have you forgotten what it's like to see the sun? To feel it on your skin – even if it is through a glass pane?'

'I don't know what's got into you Edin. You're sounding shrill.'

'Nothing's got into me. But I wonder about the rest of you. It's like you've all caught some kind of disease: no one seems to care any more about anything other than work.'

'Calm down. I was just teasing. You're blowing this way out of proportion.'

'Whatever. Have a nice night. It's going to be a long one.' I started to walk out and her voice followed me.

'Okay, okay! Just wait up a second Edin.' I heard her sigh. 'What exactly did you have in mind?'

I turned around. 'I was going down to the cafeteria to watch the sunset and have a drink. I was going to invite you to join me. That's all.'

'Well give me a few minutes to finish this report and I will.'

'I wouldn't want to tear you away from your work.'

'Stop sulking already. Go down there, pour yourself a shot and one for me. I'll join you in five.' Leila looked down at her screen and started to type. Noticing that I was still in the doorway she looked up and waved me away. 'Go on – shoo. I'll be there. I promise.'

I turned and walked off into the corridor, the after-image of Leila frowning, leaning over her monitor, burnt into my retina. I was fairly certain I'd made a huge mistake. And yet part of me was strangely elated. The conversation – as strained as it was – seemed to be some kind of breakthrough.

I just wasn't entirely sure if it would be worth it.

A distant sun

The cafeteria was deserted as I walked in. As I suspected, the others were either still working or had gone to their quarters. I could see the distant sun setting – or rather, I could see a bright patch in the hazy tangerine strip along the horizon. If you looked closely, you could just make out a disc: so tiny it was barely more than a star. The surrounding sky was already shrouded in a heavy darkness.

For a change, the outline of a partially silhouetted Saturn hung overhead, its silver likeness twinkling on the inky surface of Kraken Mare. I knew from experience that this would be brief – Titan's ubiquitous smog would soon roll in and blot it all out.

'Last chance to see, eh?'

I was startled to hear Tad's voice behind me. I turned and said: 'Yeah… The darkness is coming in fast.'

'That's winter for you. Luckily we won't be here at solstice. By then this place will barely get fifteen hours of daylight per cycle. If you can call it 'daylight'…'

'Twilight is better than no light,' I replied turning back to the view.

'You know, they reckon the lake could grow by a third. It's grown even since I've been here. I'm thinking it could get uncomfortably close to the substation.'

I didn't want to encourage him, so I said nothing. Of

all the people to run into, it had to be Tad – the only one who liked to talk. And talk. Apparently he also had some fairly recent history with Leila. That was something I found hard to believe: what the hell was that about? Her relationship with Konrad... now that was something I could understand: alpha male and all that. But Tad...

Whichever way it went, I had to get rid of him. Because I knew that if he stayed, Leila certainly wouldn't.

'You're off to your quarters now I suppose,' I said without taking my eyes off the view. I deliberately framed it as a statement – Tad was so easily led I wagered he'd take the autosuggestion and leave.

'Actually I was planning to hang around here and have a drink,' he said, laughing with a slight tremor in his voice. I felt a knot forming in my stomach. Then he continued: 'Sadly, I have to close off the perimeter wall before the temperature drops any lower. I normally do it at around half past five on the day of nightfall but today I couldn't. For some reason, Marta and Konrad are still out there.'

'Where? At the substation?'

'Yeah. You know – Marta's doing routine ops on the power supply. Konrad's collecting some of the atmospheric samples he and I have been testing.'

I checked my watch. 'Hmm. They should have been back at least half an hour ago. I wonder what's keeping them?'

'Dunno. I'm heading to the hangar now to find out. Care to tag along? I could do with the company.'

'No – I reckon I'll stay here mate. Take in the last view. Have a drink and hit the sack early. It's been a long day.'

'Oh. Okay. Well, I suppose I'll catch you later then.'

'Uh, yeah. Sure.' I smiled weakly as I caught Tad's eye. 'Oh, and make sure they come in straight away. No more delays. We can't risk it getting much darker.'

He nodded and shuffled off.

Once the door to the stairwell had closed I heard myself sighing audibly. Then I went to the liquor cabinet and carefully poured two shots, watching the single bubble of liquid roll slowly into each glass. I was carrying them to a table near the window as Leila came in from the corridor.

'Now that's exactly what I need.' I watched her glide up to the seat and slink into it. She'd tied her hair back and washed her hands and face – her cheeks were scrubbed red and I could see a bubble of water clinging to the back of her hand as she lifted the glass to her lips. She closed her eyes as she swallowed. 'Ah. It burns. And tastes like hospital cleaner. But so good anyway.'

'It's not like we can get crates of wine delivered here.'

'No. I suppose not.'

We sat in a silence for a while and watched the sunset. They last a lot longer on Titan than on Earth.

'So. What do you want to talk about?' Leila said eventually. She took another sip. 'Apart from work and video games.' She gasped a little as she gulped her drink.

I shrugged my shoulders. 'The weather?' I gestured to the window. A fog was settling in and droplets of liquid methane started to slap the glass. Leila snorted. Then she drained her glass, gasping a little more. It looked like she was about to stand up when I said: 'You just missed Tad.'

'Oh.' She stiffened visibly and settled back down in her chair.

'Don't worry – he's gone down to the hangar. Something about Konrad and Marta still being out at the substation.'

'Wow. They're running late.'

'Yes. And of course Tad can't close the perimeter wall for the night until they get in.'

'Hmm. I wonder what they're up to…' Leila's mouth curled up at the corner as she said this.

'You can't be serious!'

'Why not? Konrad and I made use of the substation once.'

'Come on…'

'Really! It offers privacy. The walls between the quarters here are paper thin. Or hadn't you noticed?'

'Believe me, I've noticed. That's why I can't believe they would bother – everyone seems so used to having zero privacy.'

Leila shrugged and extended her glass. 'A change is as good as a holiday. Top up?' I drained my own glass, took hers and headed to the cabinet.

'How long were you and Konrad… together?'

'Oh, we were never 'together'. He's a difficult man. I realised that pretty much straight away.'

'You know what I mean.'

'We had sex for about a week, if that's what you're asking. Then I got tired of him.'

'And Tad?' I brought back her drink which she took from me without making eye contact.

'Can we change the subject please?'

'There's always the weather.'

'You know…' She paused and shook her head. 'You can be a real arsehole.'

After that we sat in silence with Leila looking down running her finger around the rim of her glass. I noticed her bringing a finger up quickly to wipe an eye.

'I'm sorry. He hurt you. I didn't know.'

'He didn't hurt me. I hurt me. There's a difference.'

'You don't have to say any more. I didn't mean to pry.' Another uncomfortable silence ensued. Eventually I said: 'No one tells you much when you get to a place like this.

Not about what's really happening. You're an outsider. The group dynamics are so strange. I've been here for a month and I still feel like I don't know any of you.'

'I'm afraid we've gotten to know each other too well. It's suffocating. And disappointing. You lose all faith in humanity.'

I decided to change the subject slightly and said: 'So tell me what you know about Konrad and Marta. How long have they been an item?'

'A while. A total of three months maybe? Yes, about that.'

'Are they close?'

'They argue – a lot. But yes, I suppose they are. They're closer than anyone else here is. You would have noticed how Marta never left Konrad's side when he had that fever a few days ago.'

'You get along with the others – I mean Max and Sandra?'

'Well enough. Max, Sandra and Marta were in the first crew, as you know. I followed with Tad and Konrad. Then you came…'

'With two others who didn't make it.'

Leila nodded. 'No one said this job was for the faint-hearted, did they?' I tried to catch her eye as she said this, but Leila was staring into middle distance again.

Abruptly someone's pager started to buzz. I searched for mine then remembered I'd left it on my bed. Leila picked hers out of her pocket: 'Max? Yes, what is it? No – I don't know where Tad is. Edin says he went down to the hangar. He was going to radio Konrad and Marta… Maybe he left his pager somewhere… He's not answering the hangar radio either? Yes I know the perimeter walls need to come up… Okay, okay… Edin and I will go down and check what's happening…'

What doesn't kill you

'What was all that about?'

'That was Max. He's up in the control room and noticing the temperature plummeting outside while the perimeter wall is still down. Bloody Tad isn't answering his calls. Probably has headphones in his ears while watching porn.'

'Too much information.'

'Oh grow up.' Leila drained her glass and stood up. 'Coming? I sure as hell don't want to have to speak to the idiot alone.'

'Did Max say whether there was any sign of Konrad and Marta?'

'According to the logs, Tad opened the airlock about fifteen minutes ago. That must have been them coming back.'

'Seems to me people are starting to get a bit slack around here with the protocols.'

'You should talk.'

'What do you mean?'

'Mr 'Knock Off Early'.'

'That's unfair. I get my work done.'

'Yeah, yeah,' Leila said while checking her watch. 'Come on – get up. Let's find out what they're doing down there then close that damn wall before we lose any more heat and have to start using our backup fuel.'

I reluctantly got to my feet. Even with one seventh gravity I felt quite happy to be sitting – particularly after a few drinks. The room started to spin as I followed Leila. 'By the way, I resent your implication,' I said to her retreating back.

'Which one?'

'You know very well which one: that I somehow have a poor work ethic.'

'Oh boo hoo. You'll get over it. Or you won't.' She was speaking without looking back.

'Are you always like this?'

She paused at the door and turned around, glaring. 'Like what? Honest?'

'Brutal.'

'I told you: I'm here to work, not socialise.'

'Yet you still came down for a drink with me…'

'Listen,' she said while putting one hand on the doorknob and prodding me in the chest with the other, 'I was being kind. Whatever ideas you had when you started hitting on me, forget them. Oh, and don't go all 'puppy dog' on me like you're starting to now. It won't work. I had one guy here try that already. Waste of time. I see I've hurt your feelings. Good. Maybe you'll leave me the hell alone.'

'And there I was thinking we were getting along so nicely.'

'Ha, ha.' Her face contorted into a cross between a grimace and a smile. 'You should have gone into stand-up comedy instead of engineering. Your talents are wasted out here.' She opened the door and walked into the stairwell. I followed her.

'Or maybe I should have become a counsellor. I can see I had it right the first time: you've been hurt badly. You can try all you like to cover it up with your 'tough girl' act but it doesn't fool me.'

'Spare me the psychobabble.'

'And I think you're lashing out at me because you're stressed.'

'Why would I be stressed?'

'Because you have to confront Tad…'

'Oh shut up. What the hell do you want from me anyway?'

'Just to be your friend.'

'Thanks but I have enough friends.'

'Where?' I asked, opening my arms, my voice echoing down the stairwell. Leila simply shook her head and leapt down the steel grid frame, floating all the way to the first landing. I idly wondered why they bothered building the stairs to such an earthly design. Who thought up these things? I floated after her.

'Wait up. Let me deal with Tad.'

'Good grief. I'm not as thin-skinned as you seem to think. Besides, everything is good for you – if it doesn't kill you. In this case it'll do me some good to give him a bit of a tongue lashing.' When she reached the bottom, she pressed a button to deactivate the hermetic seal and disappeared into the hanger. I arrived just as the door clicked shut in my face.

The air in the hangar was frigid and had the lingering scent – indeed taste – of bitter almonds. I felt the goosebumps rising on my arms as I breathed out steam. Leila was already at the console, keying in something. I cast a glance around the room. Both gliders were missing.

'That airlock opening… That wasn't Konrad and Marta coming back – it was Tad going out!'

'No shit, Sherlock. The question is why.'

'Konrad's glider must have failed. Tad's gone out to get

them.'

'Except he should be back by now. It only takes ten minutes to get to the substation. Fifteen, tops.' Leila pressed some more keys then slapped the bench top. 'I've been through all the logs. Tad hasn't left any record of what's happened. No voice message, nothing.'

'Well I'll radio him,' I said, reaching for the hand-held transceiver hanging on the wall. I switched it on, pressed the call button.

'Hanger calling Glider 2, do you copy?'

But after more than a dozen attempts on all channels I was still greeted with mere white noise.

Outside the methane rain lashed the hangar door and the wind howled. Through the plexiglass I could see the strip of marmalade sky thinning – and the smog gathering its heavy cloak.

Be home soon

The thing about our base was its size. You're probably getting some idea that we had plenty of room but the reality was something altogether different. The habitat, set into the side of a cliff, comprised three connected prefab modules stacked on top of each other, each with narrow corridors, low ceilings and tiny box rooms. The 'cafeteria' in the central module was the only open area – and even that wasn't large: you could squeeze in the full complement of nine crew, but only if you really had to. Luckily (or unluckily) we seven rarely gathered together all at the same time. The rest of the floor was taken up by our cramped living quarters.

The lower module consisted of the hangar and workshop with a perspex tunnel to the greenhouse. The upper housed the infirmary, a couple of labs and of course the control room which, along with the cafeteria, offered you the only decent view of the outside. Not that there was much to see on most days – the mustard smog was usually impenetrable.

Tonight was no different in this regard. I was looking out at the view from the control room as Leila and I spoke with Max. Even though the sun hadn't yet fallen below the horizon, it was visible only as a mere pinhead of shimmering amber in circle of brown haze – a circle I could cover with my thumb. Everything else was in total blackness. It looked like a distant campfire on moonless, starless open plain back home.

'Okay, I've finally managed to log the movement of both gliders using the GPS coordinates,' said Max. 'We had a satellite signal drop out but it's back now.'

'So where are they?' Leila pulled up Max's chair and slumped into it, yawning as she spoke.

'Glider 1 is at the substation. It went directly there and hasn't moved since. I'm assuming it has broken down. Glider 2 on the other hand first headed out to the node on the lake edge. Tad must have decided to pick up his last lot of samples – even though I told him not to. From there he followed the shoreline to the inlet, then turned south to the substation.' Max was pointing to the screen, showing the routes, the first marked in red the other in yellow. I was looking over his shoulder. Leila had draped her long legs over the arm of the chair, put a limp arm on her forehead and closed her bruised eyes.

'Where is he now? Still at the substation?' I asked.

'Actually it looks like Glider 2 might be moving – heading back to base. I'll know for certain when the screen refreshes. There it is. And… yes, he's moving!'

'Hooray,' said Leila in a slurred voice, her eyes still closed.

'How long till he gets here?'

'I'd say about twelve minutes judging by his speed. Edin my dear boy, will you go down in a while and see them in – check that everyone's okay? Call me if they need medical assistance. Sandra's sleeping but I can rouse her if need be.'

'For sure Max.'

Leila opened her eyes with what appeared to be some considerable effort, pulled herself up to her feet and announced: 'Since the 'crisis' – such as it was – is now over, I think it's safe to assume my presence is no longer required. I'm going to lie down.'

'You do that my dear,' said Max. 'We can manage things from here.'

'Good. Because I have the worst headache I've ever had.'

'Need anything for that?'

'You bet your life. Got some codeine?'

'That bad?'

'That bad.'

'Hmm.' Max opened his desk drawer and took out a box which he flicked to Leila. It floated gently through the thick air and she caught it with both hands — a little too roughly so that the box was partially crushed in her grip. 'Buprenorphine,' said Max. 'Don't swallow them: they dissolve under your tongue. Don't take more than one at a time,' he warned. 'And for God's sake, let's see if we can fix the air supply system. We can't all keep breathing hydrogen cyanide — even if the concentrations are low.'

'Yeah, yeah. You don't think I know that? I installed new filters yesterday. I'll take some air samples tomorrow morning and test them. See if there's been any improvement. Good night.'

'Rest well and I hope you feel better soon,' Max replied. I said nothing.

Leila, who was already staggering to the door like a drunk, gave us a slow 'royal wave' over her shoulder but didn't look back.

When she had gone I turned to Max and said: 'She's got quite a bite, that woman.'

'You've only just noticed?'

'I asked her to join me for a drink at sunset. Which she did — after a bit of a fight. Then when we went down to the hangar she picked up the argument where she left off before. She sure punches above her weight. And below the belt.'

'Hmm. That sounds about right. What was the fight about?' Max was regarding me intently as he spoke. I couldn't tell if he was smiling or not.

He was the oldest in our group: peppercorn hair and moustache, laugh lines around his eyes, hair that I'm pretty sure would have been like Einstein's had Sandra not cut it regularly. I wanted to spend more time with him as he seemed genuinely likeable – but he was also deeply eccentric and hard to read.

'The fight? I don't really know. Something about my poor work ethic. Or the fact that I was hitting on her – which I wasn't.'

Max chuckled. 'You're a bad liar.'

'Maybe. But I'd like to think I'm a polite one.'

'Well, all I can say is that it's clear she's attracted to you.'

'What the hell are you talking about Max? We practically came to blows. Over nothing.'

'And?'

'That's not normally a sign of interest.'

'What planet are you from?' laughed Max. 'It's always a sign of interest. Indifference is the sign of disinterest.'

'Well this 'interest' comes with a different intention.'

'I wouldn't put too much stock in 'intention' my dear lad. For example, in the Vietnam War one out of five American soldiers admitted to being addicted to heroin.'

'Sorry Max – what has that got to do with…'

'Let me finish. Do you know how many stayed addicts when they got back home? About five percent. That means ninety five percent of the former addicts got clean at home – and stayed that way.'

'Why are you telling me this?'

'Because intention has little or nothing to do with what people actually do. You can intend to change your life all you want. It won't happen until you change your environment – be it physical, emotional, whatever. The soldiers only got clean when they went home. And they were only addicts when they were at war. They changed when their environment changed. Not when their 'intentions' changed.'

'You mean she was biting my head off because of where we were?'

'Where, with whom… all of that.'

'I told her she was pissed off at Tad and taking it out on me.'

'Don't forget Konrad.'

'I suppose him too. But that still doesn't mean she's interested in me…'

'I'm afraid it does, my dear Edin.'

'Why?'

'You, Tad and Konrad – you all get the same reaction because you're all part of the 'environment' that provokes it. Which leads me to deduce that she's attracted to you in much the same way as she was attracted to both of them.'

'Somehow I don't find that comforting.'

'The truth rarely is.'

'It sounds like you're blaming me for her bad temper.'

'No. I'm just saying that, whether you like it or not, you are bad for her. At least right now – in her current state. And in your current state. You're the environment she needs to change. She's like those soldiers in Vietnam. She needs to go home. And she needs to do it soon.'

'I know you're a doctor Max. And I generally like you. But sometimes you're full of shit.'

A sudden beeping sounded in the control room and Max turned to the console.

'Glider 2 is inside the perimeter gate. And just in the nick of time too. We're losing the last light. Now be a good boy, run down and find out what all the fuss was about. Buzz me when you see them and I'll shut the outer wall from here. And ask Tad why the hell he hasn't answered his radio.'

Something strong

I stopped by my room to pick up my pager. I knew I had enough time: getting through the airlock wasn't exactly something you could do quickly. But when I got to the hangar, Tad hadn't even started the procedure. He seemed to be parked outside waiting for me. I guess that's when I first started to worry: nothing was making sense – the strange delays, the radio silence, and now this. I grabbed my transceiver.

'Glider 2 do you copy, over?' Silence. 'Okay Tad, Konrad, Marta – if you can hear me, I'm activating the airlock now. Pull in and wait for the green light.' More silence.

I started the process in a bit of a panic. Then I realised that Tad's transceiver doubled as an airlock remote. Something had to be wrong with it. This would also explain the radio silence. So I allowed myself to breathe again as I waited for countdown to finish.

After the vacuum phase I heard the gradual rush of gas as the atmosphere equalised with the exterior, then the creak and groan of the hangar doors opening.

The outside floodlights were on and I could see the glider sitting dark and mute at the entrance, drizzled in methane rain. Abruptly the glider's headlights flashed on, I heard its electric engine whirring and saw it lurch forward into the hangar.

If Tad was piloting the craft, he was doing so badly: he hadn't waited for the door to open fully, so I winced as it narrowly missed scraping its roof. I watched through the plexiglass window on the door as it inched forwards in stops and starts, finishing far too close to the back wall. Then the engine and headlights cut out.

I was reaching for my pager to call Max when the mother of all explosions rocked the entire building – I saw the plastic-shelled, inflated walls flex acutely from the shock, which in turn caused an internal wave that tossed my light body into the air. The lights flickered and went out, plunging everything into utter blackness.

I was floating in the dark for at least a second, completely disoriented. Was I up or down? Then the middle of my back collided with something sharp: the edge of a stair. After that my head bashed into the central pole, the loud clang echoing up the well. I could feel the steel grid meshwork as my hip bounced on it and, half a second later, the wind being knocked out of me as I hit the cold floor and slid along it. My boots made a hollow sound as they collided with a wall.

I lay there for quite a while in the darkness. My head started to ache just above and behind my temple – a sharp point of pain with a throbbing aura. I could taste iron in my mouth. My tongue chased down the gash on the inside of my cheek.

The power snapped on again. The backup generator.

I heard the distant sounds of something pelting the roof and perimeter wall. I got to my knees and then, somewhat uncertainly, to my feet. My hands searched frantically for the pager which had been clipped to my hip. Eventually I saw it lying at the base of the first step. I picked it up, fumbled it in the air and watched it spiral downwards casually. I grabbed it again and, with trembling, clumsy fingers, punched in Max's three digit PIN.

'Max!'

'Edin.'

'What the fuck just happened? It seems like…'

'The substation exploded. I happened to be watching the last of the sunset, waiting for your call. Saw the whole thing blow sky-high. Tell me, are you in one piece?'

'Yes – I think so. Smacked my head a bit but I'm okay.'

'And the people in the glider?'

'All quiet,' I said, walking up to the door rubbing my head. A lump was rising. My hand came away sticky and wet. The glider had its nose pushed into the wall, striations running through the plastic of both. 'There's no sign of movement.'

'I wonder if they're all in there?'

'I hope so. What about the others? Sandra and Leila?'

'They've just staggered in. They look a bit shocked but seem to be okay. The control room is a bit of a mess – the low gravity means everything gets thrown about easily. Right now, the priority is to get those people out of the glider,' said Max.

'Can we close the airlock when we're on the generator?'

'Yes, that shouldn't matter. It'll just take a moment to reboot the system. Is the glider intact?'

'It seems to have rammed the wall a bit, but it looks solid enough. Probably have to change the front panels.'

'Okay, that's good. Listen, the system's just rebooted, so run the airlock. We're coming down with the medivac. Expect the worst.'

I went to the console and pressed the flashing start button. Thankfully it had cached the last procedure and everything continued from where it had left off. I heard the hangar door creak, saw it shudder. For a moment I thought it might be jammed. Then it started to grind its way down into place until the hermetic seal clicked. The extractor fans began to whine. After a while fresh air began to blast into the hangar.

Max and the others were opening the door at the top of the stairwell just as the light flashed green. I didn't wait for them but opened the door.

The frozen, bitter air hit me like a full body tackle – my throat and lungs spasmed and I heard myself gasp involuntarily. I lunged for the glider hatch, pulling at the frozen handle which jammed at first, then suddenly gave way causing me to slip and spin around. I felt some skin tearing off my palm.

When I recovered my balance I saw that Tad was in the pilot's seat. The rest of the glider was empty. He was bleeding profusely from a cut somewhere under his matted hair and smiled at me weakly without moving.

'What took you so long?'

As he finished saying this, the door to the stairwell burst open. I heard Max shouting.

Falling down

I scrambled into the cockpit next to Tad. At first I didn't realise that he had his seatbelt fastened. Once I undid that, I put my hand behind his shoulder and tried to help him up out of his seat, but he stayed limp like a sack of potatoes. Max suddenly materialised and motioned for me to move aside. When I withdrew my hand it came away thick blood all the way up my sleeve. I had somehow thought the wetness was just sweat caused by the dense, moist air of the glider.

I crawled over to the copilot seat and Max pulled out a penlight torch and crouched down next to Tad who was still grinning like a loon.

'Tad, can you understand what I'm saying?' Max was trying to look into his eyes but Tad was lolling his head from side to side. I saw a pulse on the back of his head behind his temple, like a mini volcano, blood oozing out on a one second beat onto his matted hair.

'He's bleeding...'

I heard Sandra's voice behind me say: 'Put this on it.' She was thrusting a rolled up bandage at me. I took it and jammed it into the wound, clip and all, pressing hard.

'What a ride!' Tad said abruptly. 'Seriously. You guys don't know it yet, but you soon will. Nothing is ever going to be the same.' His eyes went wide as he looked at me, gesticulating. 'How can it be?'

'Listen to me,' said Max, holding his chin with his fingers so as to keep his head still. 'Can you tell me your name?'

'Tadeuz Jesnoewski,' he said through pinched cheeks.

'Do you know where you are?'

'In the glider, of course.'

'What day is it?'

'Uh… Day four of the twenty-fifth cycle. It's the end of the day. In your time, that is,' he chuckled. 'In real time – well that's a bit complicated.'

I looked quizzically at Max but he just shook his head. He turned back to Tad and said, with careful enunciation: 'Alright, we're going to help you onto the stretcher. Understand? Before we do that I need to know where you're hurt.'

'Konrad stabbed me with a screwdriver. Right here.' He pointed to where I had the bandage pressed to his head.

'Are you injured anywhere else? Have you hurt your back or neck?'

'Uh, they're fine.' He adjusted himself a bit in his seat. 'Maybe a bit bruised.'

'Where are Konrad and Marta?'

'Hm? Oh. They're dead. In your time, anyway.'

'Are you sure?'

'Yeah man. When I got there, Konrad… he'd already killed Marta. He tried to kill me but I got away. Now he's blown up the whole substation. He said he was going to do it. I didn't know why then, but I'm starting to see it, you know? He had to do it. To escape.'

'Escape what?'

'This…' he gestured around himself. 'I mean, it's pretty shitty, isn't it? Your environment affects everything. Sometimes you've got to do something pretty drastic.'

'So you're sure he and Marta didn't get away in the other glider?'

Tad started to laugh, but lapsed into a coughing fit. When he recovered he said: 'Yeah, I'm sure. Marta was lying there all white and cold. Her blood was, like, all over the place. And Konrad said he wasn't coming back. He scuttled the first glider, you know? Broke the windshield and put holes in the fuselage.'

'Listen Tad, we're going to help you get up now. Can you try to stand?'

'Okay.' He gingerly raised himself with Max's and my help.

Once outside, Max and I picked him up, me at his shoulders and Max at his feet, and we placed him on the stretcher that Sandra and Leila had unfolded and pulled parallel to the glider. Sandra had taken over holding the rolled up bandage against Tad's head. By now the blood had soaked all the way through. The air in the hangar had warmed up but it was still not that much different to a commercial meat freezer. I thought it would probably help stem the blood flow a little.

Leila leaned over him and said: 'Tad – are you absolutely sure Konrad and Marta are dead?'

Tad just smiled serenely and closed his eyes.

The hardest part about the stairs was getting the stretcher around the corners – it felt a bit like moving furniture. Thankfully the low gravity made things a lot easier than it might have been – although we'd all lost a lot of muscle too. I nearly bumped Tad's head into the central pole a couple of times.

Eventually we got him up to the infirmary and shifted him into a bed. No sooner had we done this, than I started to see stars. Leila was standing near me and said:

'You're looking a bit pale. Are you okay?'

'I think so.'

'Let me see. Jesus. That blood on you can't all be Tad's.'

'No, some of it's mine. Banged my head earlier.' My vision was starting to narrow into a tunnel. A loud hum was welling in my ears, drowning out Leila's voice.

'You'd better sit down. Max! Sandra!'

'No, I think I'll be fine. I just need some water. My throat is so dry.'

That was the last thing I remembered.

I was sitting up in bed being treated by Sandra when Max popped his head in.

'How's the other patient?'

'He's okay. Fainted on us. Luckily Leila caught him before he smacked his head again. He's got a bit of a cut on the back of his scalp. And a pretty big lump which we've been icing. I'm about to stitch the wound with some glue,' said Sandra. 'He's also lost some skin off one of his palms. 'I stared down at my bandaged hand as she said this. 'Otherwise he's okay.'

I was in the second infirmary bed. Tad was in the first. He'd been babbling away but had stopped some time before.

'How's Tad doing Max?' I asked.

'Thankfully he's fallen asleep. Sandra, we'll have to monitor his vital signs carefully.' She merely nodded.

'What's wrong with him?'

'He's concussed. It's making him confused. Head trauma does that. Looks like he was hit quite a few times, apart from the stab with the screwdriver. It must have been a hell of a fight.'

'Has he lost a lot of blood?'

'It's better than it looks. He should be okay.'

'Max, what are we going to do?'

I stretched to turn around but Sandra gave me a slap on the shoulder saying: 'Don't do that, you idiot! I'm almost done. You'll wreck it.'

'Let's not worry about things Edin,' Max replied. 'We'll have a group meeting in the morning and make a plan. Right now I'm going to shut down all the non-essential services to preserve power. We'll get through this. Remember, the launch vehicle has fuel too, which we can use if we have to. As I say, we'll talk about it in the morning.' He winked and gave me a smile. I heard the door click as he left.

'There,' said Sandra, clapping her hands. 'Good as new.'

She was a lithe woman, bronze hair, a full lips and fair, freckled porcelain skin. It was hard not to like her, but she was also quite reserved. She was more inclined to make the odd witty observation than be the life and soul of the party.

'What do you think Sandy – is Tad going to be okay?'

She raised her eyebrows, then turned to pack away her equipment. 'Oh – God knows.'

'Surely he's just been banged in the head.'

'Yes. But then again…'

'Then again what?'

Sandra shook her head. 'I shouldn't speculate. Let's leave it and see in the morning.'

'Come on – seriously. I want to know.'

Sandra sighed deeply. 'It's nothing really. I've probably got it all wrong.'

'Tell me!'

'I just think Tad was losing it before all this happened. And I wonder whether he hasn't finally snapped.'

'Oh…'

'He's been getting stranger and stranger. Leila broke it off with him because of that. Since then he seems to have been getting steadily worse. Max had to give him anti-depressants.' Sandra abruptly waved her hand in front of her face. 'But I've said too much.'

I nodded. 'Okay. Lips sealed. I won't repeat anything. Can you tell me more about Konrad?'

Sandra winced. 'He was always a loose cannon. You could see he had a potential for violence. We all should have seen this coming. Especially in the way he treated Marta…'

'I thought they got along. I mean, Leila said they were close.'

'Close? Maybe. But he was getting more and more unstable. And he was taking it out on Marta. She stayed loyal to him though. When Leila and I told her to break it off with him, she stopped talking to us. That was around the time you arrived. We three used to be quite close.'

'I'm starting to get the picture why the dynamics of this place are so weird.'

'By the way, Konrad was insanely jealous of Tad and Leila: he was always quietly simmering over it. I was pretty sure he still had a thing for Leila but he was using Marta in the meantime. We all breathed a sigh of relief when Leila finally broke it off with Tad. We were worried Konrad would kill him. The fact that they were meant to work together on the cultures just made it worse. Max always had to set the schedules so that there was a third person around. As it happens, we even told Tad not to go out this afternoon. God knows why he did.'

'Presumably to see what happened to Konrad and Marta. Speaking of which, what do you think happened out there?'

'Konrad finally lost it, obviously. And killed Marta.' For

the first time since I'd known Sandra her usually impeccable façade was starting to crack. I saw her bottom lip tremble and she looked away, back to her equipment, which she made a show of sorting. 'Then Tad happened along,' she said, without turning around, her voice wavering.

I sat in silence for a while. Eventually I said: 'I never saw any of this coming.'

'Looking back now, I should have,' Sandra replied. She grabbed a tissue and blew her nose. 'Which is why I'm worried about Tad.'

'What do you mean? He's not violent – is he?'

'Tad? Heavens no! It's just that…'

'Go on.'

'He's sounding a lot like Konrad did before he and Marta left for the substation.'

'How?'

'Well Konrad was acting weird. He and poor Marta were heading down to the hangar and I stopped them for a chat. I wanted to check up on her, obviously. But she still wasn't talking to me. So I ended up talking to Konrad. He didn't make any sense at all. He started talking about relativity and quantum mechanics – saying something about how time is 'just imaginary'. Quoting Einstein. It seemed totally random. And he was saying it all with that stupid smile of his. I just thought he was playing some kind of game with me. Being a prick, as usual. But I can see now that something was wrong. I'm afraid something similar is wrong with Tad.'

'Listen Sandra, I'm no psychologist. But it sounds to me like Tad's just repeating stuff Konrad was saying at the substation – maybe during the attack. His head is scrambled.'

'I'm sure you're right,' she said. She headed for the

door where she paused. 'It's been a long evening. I'm off to bed. Call me if you need anything.'

I nodded and tried to give her an encouraging smile. I could see her eyes were bloodshot. I wondered whether I should do something – like give her a hug – but it felt too awkward. And then she was gone.

Not who you think you are

Max and Sandra had wanted me to stay in the infirmary overnight, but it didn't seem at all necessary. I wanted to sleep in my own bed. Besides, I didn't much like the idea of Tad in the bed next to mine, separated by nothing more than a curtain. He might have been an invalid at this point, but I was still freaked out by what I'd heard. So I disconnected the monitoring pads and crept past his bed. I couldn't hear him at all. I wondered if he was wide awake – maybe listening.

It was strange walking down the empty corridor in the relative darkness – only the green emergency lights were on. The same was the case throughout the habitat. My head was pounding from the blow – I'd never known a headache like it. I also felt nausea, almost certainly from concussion.

I thought of waking Max or Sandra. But for all I knew they were on shifts to look after Tad – I might wake the wrong one. I also didn't want them to hassle me into going back to the infirmary. It would be easier if they found me gone – they'd know I'd crawled into my own bed and would probably leave me alone. After all, Tad was the one who was genuinely unwell.

I tiptoed past their rooms, wondering for the umpteenth time whether they ever slept together. No one ever said anything to suggest that, but at the same time they seemed very close.

I paused outside Leila's room. I knew she had some of Max's painkillers and I wondered if I should ask her for one. I'll confess I also had other, ill-formed, reasons for calling on her. However in the end when I raised my hand to knock, it faltered and withdrew. I realised I'd had enough drama for one day.

Back in my room I took a long shower, washing the smell of blood, antiseptic and bitter almonds off my skin and out of my hair. I saw myself in the mirror by the ghostly green emergency light: I was pale and thin, muscle wasted from the low gravity. I had bags under my eyes and I needed to shave. The pad on my hand was now wet and heavy. I tried to dry it by dabbing it with a towel, but was only partially successful and eventually I gave up.

I must have brushed my teeth for ten full minutes, avoiding the cuts on the inside of my cheek. Somehow I couldn't get the taste of the hangar out of my mouth. And whenever I closed my eyes I saw the afterglow of blood, both fresh and dried – the little speckles that people get all over their faces and bodies – particularly in low gravity – the trembling of Tad's alabaster limbs as we lifted him.

Most of all I kept thinking about what we were going to do to survive. Even with the most conservative energy use it seemed we would run out of fuel in a matter of days. The second substation was weeks away from completion. I was meant to be working on it with Konrad, but he'd delayed and delayed. Somehow there was always a higher priority. It would only be needed by the time the next crews arrived anyway, he said. Now we'd have to wait for light before we resumed work on it – and that was at least eleven or so days away.

As I crawled into bed I started calculating how long we had before we ran out of generator fuel. I was running through the figures but drawing a blank when I tried to factor in the variables – essential services use only, lowering the thermostat, moving to one level over the period of darkness. My mind kept being interrupted by an odd mixture of pain and the drift into uneasy sleep, yet I felt that I was just about to solve the problem.

I started dreaming without realising it. I was back in university, doing some sort of exam – physics, specifically quantum mechanics and string theory. The invigilator smacked me on the head with a stick. I wanted to tell him I was busy working something out. But he smacked me on the same spot. And kept smacking – rhythmically: one… two… three… A pause. Then he resumed. I started raising a hand to stop him, but I was too weak. When I opened my mouth, no words came out. The pain from the blows was excruciating.

Suddenly I woke up. It was dark except for the green exit light. I waited there holding my breath, wondering what had happened. My head was still pulsing to the beat of the ache.

And I heard it again: someone was knocking on my door – a slow knock – one… two… three… matching the pulse in my head.

In a startle, I shuffled my feet, knocking the covers off. I watched them float down to the floor.

'Who's there?' I whispered. But there was no answer.

I shuffled to the edge of my bed and whispered again. 'Sandra? Tad?'

'It's me.'

Of course that meant nothing. I didn't recognise the voice at all, although it sounded like a woman. So, with heart still pounding, I carefully opened the door, hearing the hermetic seal click.

It took me a moment to recognise the shadow.

'Leila?'

'You were sleeping. I'm sorry. I thought you might still be up.'

'No, no, it's alright. What's happening?'

'I couldn't sleep so I went by the infirmary and noticed you were gone.'

'Yeah – I wanted to sleep in my own bed.'

'How are you?' Her voice was surprisingly soft. Somehow she looked much smaller and more vulnerable in the dark, her arms crossed and hugging herself.

'Uh, okay. Actually no. I've got the headache from hell.'

'You should have asked. I have plenty of Max's tablets left. You want me to go and get them?'

'Yeah – sure. That would be great.'

'Okay. Hang about. I'll be back. I'll knock again. This time you'll know it's me.'

She disappeared quickly down the corridor and I retreated to my room and sat on the edge of the bed. A moment of nausea almost overwhelmed me, then passed.

Another series of soft knocks. I rose and opened the door.

'Here.' She thrust the box at me. 'You know the drill. Dissolve one in your mouth. They work a treat.'

'Okay. Thanks.'

'Can I come in?'

'Oh, yes of course. Please do. I'm sorry. I've forgotten my manners.'

I stepped aside and she seemed to slide in – almost in a panic. Her arms were still crossed tightly at her chest. I let the door click shut and watched her as she stood to one side of the green exit light, her lips pursed tightly. She smelled of soap and freshly shampooed hair. I didn't say anything, so I opened the box and peeled back one of the tabs to reveal a crumbly tablet.

'Remember – under your tongue.'

'Yes ma'am,' I said, and put one in my mouth. She just watched me. 'Everything okay Leila?' I said, as clearly as one can when one has something in one's mouth. I felt the acidic taste and a slight fizz. It tasted similar to dissolvable aspirin. I threw the box onto my bedside table.

'Yes. No. It's been a shit day.'

'You can say that again.'

She didn't reply but stared down at her feet.

'Can I do anything for you?' I said at last.

'Would you mind awfully if I stayed here tonight?'

'Um. No. Not if you really want...'

'Don't get any ideas – okay? I just don't want to be alone.'

'Me neither. Except there's only one bed...'

'I know that, you idiot. You lie down on the left. I'll take the right.'

'Okay...'

She climbed in before I had a chance to finish, picking my covers off the floor and throwing them over herself. I followed after her.

'Stay on your end. And turn around.'

'Yes ma'am.' I slipped under the blanket, pulling it over but finding it stopping short. Oh well. The painkiller was starting to hit me – a rush of honey over my brain, numbing the noise and shake of the pneumatic thumping. I could feel the warmth radiating from her side of the bed. For the first time since before I went down to the hangar, I grinned.

'You know,' I said, 'you're not who you think you are.'

'Shut up.'

I chuckled and closed my eyes and fell into the sweet, full embrace of the buprenorphine.

Getting on with life

I awoke to see that Max had switched on the day lamps. Or more likely, he'd simply forgotten to make sure they didn't come on automatically. The base used a variety of compact fluorescent tubes and LEDs to cast a balanced spectrum through a line of opaque panels along the top of the bedroom walls. This simulated soft, early morning light – the kind you might get through a frosted glass window back home. It was intended to activate the body's natural clock.

An arm lay across my chest. I looked over and saw Leila sprawled on her stomach, dark eyelids closed, strands of raven hair across her face, the back of her chest rising slowly and rhythmically. I could see a few moles on her otherwise smooth skin, the plastic clip of her twisted strap, the curve of her breast, barely concealed by her slip. It occurred to me that we all kept wearing our same clothes. Some of them, like Leila's slip, were becoming distinctly threadbare. It's not as if we could run down to the local department store to replace them.

After a promising start, I'd had a terrible night's sleep. The buprenorphine might have removed most of the pain, but it also left me in a kind of twilight world, perpetually drifting off, only to be pulled back by the abrupt tautness of invisible mooring ropes.

When I thought about it, I could remember dreaming:

recurring patterns of thought that were as hard to get rid of as the narcotic hum in my ears. At times I was Konrad. And somehow Tad as well. Leila was Issy – my wife back home. I was in hospital, breaking down. Max and Sandra were treating me. Leila/Issy kept crying.

Despite this, I felt conscious enough to get up at any time. In fact, I did exactly that on several occasions in a desperate bid to try to break the cycle. By contrast, Leila had snored softly for most of the night, rolling over occasionally until the covers were twisted like rope around her waist. I left them to her and grabbed the extra blanket from the top of the wardrobe.

I smiled when, at some time in the early hours of the morning, Leila curled up behind me so that her hot breath fanned the back of my neck and I could feel the warmth of her skin. Despite an initial rise in my pulse, I soon found myself fading into the vacuum of dreamless sleep.

In the end it was a fresh pounding in my head that woke me. I looked at the bedside clock: 06:06. I'd slept properly for about two hours. I reached for the box of painkillers and opened the cardboard flap as quietly as I could. Once I'd taken a sheet out, I peeled back the foil and placed one of the wafers under my tongue. Leila stirred, lifted the hand that was on my chest, used it to scratch her nose vigorously, then put it back down, nuzzling deeper against my shoulder and momentarily squeezing my ribs with her fingers. She let out a deep sigh. I lay completely still until her breathing became rhythmic again, then gently extricated myself.

Out in the corridor the lights were still off, although I could see the white glow of the day lamps in the cafeteria. Max was straightening the furniture which had been knocked about by the explosion. I saw the small vacuum cleaner out. Leila's and my shot glasses were lying on the floor. So was an e-reader (probably Sandra's).

'Ah, Edin,' said Max. 'Good morning. I saw that you took yourself off to your own bed. How are you feeling?' He grinned from under his moustache and the corners of his eyes crinkled.

'Not too bad. I got Leila to give me some of those opiates of yours. Got rid of the pain but stuffed up my sleep.'

'Hmm. They can do that. See how you go tonight. I can give you something else if you need it.'

I nodded. 'How's Tad?' I bent down to pick up the shot glasses. One was cracked.

Max shook his head. 'We had a tough night with him. He's started burning a nasty fever. I'm giving him intravenous antibiotics. Sandra and I took shifts. He's out cold now.' Max looked down at his pager. I knew the readout would be showing Tad's vital signs.

'He'll make it, though – surely?'

Max studied the pager for a moment longer, a frown etched into his forehead. Then he clipped it back on his hip, took a deep breath and leaned on the chair he'd just straightened. 'To be honest, I don't know. But we've done as much as we can. He could be bleeding in the brain. We'd need to do a CT. But it wouldn't help much to know anyway. It's not as if we can do brain surgery out here.'

I nodded. After a while I said: 'How's the base holding up – no breaches, I take it?'

'Seems to be intact. Some of the debris pelted the roof but there are no signs of leakage from the main building. The readings from the greenhouse are offline, although I think there would be signs if its integrity were breached in any major way. I might get you to go check it out after breakfast. Take your outside suit. If there are any repairs that might need doing urgently, they'll be in there. We need our food. Can't survive on that blasted freeze-dried stuff.'

I didn't want to point out that we might not have enough of the 'blasted freeze-dried stuff' either. 'Have you sent a report home yet?'

Max grimaced. 'No. Transmitter is down. No satellite signal. I'll need you to go and take a look at the dish. Also check out the launch vehicle and make sure it's okay. Power it up and get it to run its own diagnostic.'

'I can do that.'

Max replaced an overturned jug on the main table and used a rag off his shoulder to soak up a bubble of water. 'Come help me up in the control room. That's where the real mess is.'

I felt a prod at my elbow and looked up to see Leila holding the bowl of cooked potatoes, tomatoes and diced carrot from our greenhouse. She gave me a quick smile. I nodded, took the tongs and put some of the food onto my plate. The four of us were sitting at the main table in the cafeteria. The room was quiet except for the clink of cutlery and the sound of chewing. A bleary-eyed Sandra sat opposite me, prodding at some rehydrated mix. Max was next to her. We were having the first group breakfast since my arrival.

Max seemed to read my mind and said: 'So good to be together. Feels just like old times eh?' He was grinning and the apparent morning brightness of the room and the domestic normalcy of the situation seemed to reinforce his message. But no one replied. He chewed a few more mouthfuls before adding: 'Come on people. Cheer up. We're alive and together. That's what counts.'

I took a deep breath. 'I, for one, appreciate your

positivity Max. But I guess we're worried. How are we going to stretch the fuel reserves? I keep running through the figures and I can't see a way. We can abandon the place and head for home, but the launch vehicle will only take three…'

The clinking and chewing stopped.

Max broke the silence. 'No one is going anywhere. Understood? We have about a week in reserve. Then we can switch to the fuel in the launch vehicle which buys us another week of low power use. That means we have about two weeks to finish that new substation and connect it to this habitat. We'll have to work overtime but I think we can do it. If we pull together.'

'But we have another eleven or so days of darkness…' I replied.

'We'll work by torchlight.'

'In pitch darkness, fog and driving rain?'

'We have no choice.' Max had his elbows on the table and was picking his teeth with his fingernails. 'We have the light from the glider. And there are a few backup batteries for Glider 1 that we won't be needing.'

'What about the garden Max?' asked Leila. 'Can we afford to power it now that we're on the generator? The lights use a lot of energy.'

'Thankfully the LEDs can be set to target only the spectrum of light the plants need. That means they'll drain less power. I've programmed that already: it should run as soon as the greenhouse is back online. But yes – basically, if there's one place we need to keep running, it's down there. We'll lower the thermostat and grow only the stuff that likes the cold. We keep the hangar and workshop powered but put the rest of the base in stasis. We won't be comfortable, but we'll survive.'

'You're not suggesting we move down there?'

'That's exactly what I'm suggesting. We carry down extra clothes, a bit of bedding, the freeze dried supplies and whatever else we need. No toilets, showers, nothing. We shit and piss on the garden and we use the greenhouse water for drinking.'

'What about Tad?' interrupted Sandra.

Max looked down at his linked fingers. 'The next twenty-four hours will tell. Either way, we'll be moving him down to the greenhouse with us after that. Or we won't.'

It's natural

I was in my outside suit, feeling my way along the tubular tunnel that ran from the workshop, my torch beam lighting dust particles suspended in the low gravity and my breath fogging the visor intermittently.

Up ahead I could see the greenhouse was in total darkness. Clearly something was wrong. Then I remembered that it had its own power grid which might just have tripped off.

The tunnel was in effect acting as an airlock. So when I opened the door I braced myself for a rush of air. We kept the habitat at a slightly higher pressure than the exterior so that in the event of a leak, air would seep out, rather than having the dangerous atmospheric gasses seep in. I realised that Konrad must have dropped the air pressure at the substation prior to causing a breach. All it would have taken was one ignition source, mixed with the oxygen-rich air of the substation and the incoming methane and other hydrocarbons, for the whole station to blow sky-high. He would have manually overridden all of the protections.

Thankfully there was no rush of air outward when I opened the door. The hermetic seal clicked open like any other door. I shone my torch over the deserted domes and my lonely beam caught the rows of plants in their hydroponic trays: onions, lettuce, radishes. I heard clucking at my feet and looked down to see three of our chickens investigating the sudden light source. One turned a beady eye up at me, then shied away as I shone the light directly onto it.

Abruptly my pager sounded. I had it hooked up to my suit, so I went to press the answer button, missing it the first couple of times because of my thick glove.

'Leila?'

'Hi Edin – where are you now?'

'I'm in the greenhouse. Hold on.' I admit I felt a sudden endorphin rush at hearing her voice. It stirred memories of the long, rather surreal, night before. It seemed so deeply out of place to feel excited – happy even – despite all the uncertainty of our survival. But perhaps it was only natural. I'd heard similar stories before: how the human psyche permits emotional attachments in the most stressful times – like war, or in this case, disaster.

Whichever way it went, I couldn't seem to control my emotions: I was being swept along – and enjoying the ride.

In a rush of confidence, I unlocked the seals on my helmet, heard the hiss and lifted it off, inhaling the crisp air. The greenhouse had lost a lot of its heat. I unclipped my pager and spoke directly into it. 'All looks fine. The chickens are pecking at things. No change in the air. My reader says it's six degrees. I'm guessing there's no leak – just a drop in temperature due to the power outage. I'm just moving to the control console now.'

'You've taken your helmet off, haven't you?'

'I might have.'

'You goof.' I could imagine her smiling, shaking her head.

I laughed. 'Well the chickens are fine – so why wouldn't I be? You know: canaries in coal mines and all that.'

'Okay wise guy, have it your way. Tell me: what does

the console say?'

'It's flashing. Looks like it just needs to reboot. Hold on a tick.' I held the program and reset buttons down together. After a moment the readout scrolled through the boot procedure until it read 'Online'. The lights abruptly flickered on, albeit in dull, garish colours. The ones nearest to me (over the potatoes) were a kind of neon pink. 'Yep. It's working. Tell you what, Max's colour scheme is going to make living down here very interesting.'

Leila snorted and laughed. 'Sure is. I can see it all on camera now. I can see you as well. You need to stop slouching, by the way.'

'Yes dear.'

'Oh, and I have a bit of news for you.'

'Yeah?'

'Tad's fever has broken.'

'Well thank Christ for that. Is he conscious?'

'Yes – sitting up.'

'And his mental state?'

'Not sure. I'm staying out of it. Max and Sandra have been talking to him. But from what little they've told me, he's still confused. Thinks he and I are still together.'

'Oh. A bang on the head will do that to you. At least those antibiotics did the trick.'

'Maybe. Maybe not.'

'How so?'

'The fever might have been a coincidence. Sandra reminded us that she had treated Konrad for a fever a couple of days ago – remember? It only lasted the night.'

'Of course. Any idea what that was all about?'

'No, unfortunately. I took some samples but never got around to analysing them. It was over so quickly after all. Sandra's taken a blood sample from Tad. I'm going to compare them now – do a full DNA analysis of both. See if there is any bacterial or viral infection.'

'Can't be serious either way. A twenty-four hour thing. Hey, tell Max I'm going to hang around a while and do a thorough physical check.'

'Okay. Max says don't forget to have a look at the dish and the launch vehicle.'

'Sure. I'll report later.'

'You do that.'

I spent another twenty minutes walking around checking the frame and the clear vinyl domes of the greenhouse canopy. Everything seemed to be in order. We probably had a few near misses: I could see some large, jagged pieces of plastic wall sheeting on the flat plain outside. One had missed by a matter of five metres or so.

I fed the chickens, donned my helmet, and headed for the airlock.

Outside I shone my torch through the thick fog. It only illuminated a small circle in front of me so I could barely make out the dirty water-ice 'rocks' we'd used to mark the pathway up the hill to the satellite dish. I'd been lost out here once before and it wasn't a happy experience. I consoled myself that I had the radio plugged into my suit for when I got out of range of the pager. I'd definitely need it at the launch vehicle which was resting on the plain on the other side – about a ten minute walk. Max wanted to connect its fuel tanks to the generator and I knew that wouldn't be easy. The piping would have to go around the hill. We had enough, but only just. I suppose it had always been part of a contingency plan.

I decided to go to the launch vehicle first. Happily, it was unaffected. I powered up its auxiliary system and got the computer to run a full diagnostic. This wasted about half an hour. But in the end everything was fine.

Sadly, I had no such luck with the satellite dish. It had suffered a more or less direct hit from debris. The odds seemed quite incredible. I had to pull a piece of wall sheeting off and to the side. Even in the low gravity, I started to sweat from the exertion. Finally I could see the cracked plastic and the severed wires. Still, it was clearly repairable. I thought I might get Leila's help after lunch.

So I radioed back to report the news. I was a little disappointed when Max answered.

Then I set off back into the darkness, using my headlight torch to illuminate the strategically placed marker rocks. Despite wandering off the track a couple of times I managed to find the markers again fairly quickly, and sighed with relief when I saw the glow of the greenhouse up ahead. I had a good feeling everything was going to be just as Max said. I chose to believe that even though I knew it was almost certainly just the endorphins 'talking'.

Possessed

Leila was waiting for me as I came through the airlock into the workshop. She was slouching against the wall, arms crossed, wearing a cardigan with long, floppy sleeves that extended past her hands. I waved and she gave me one of her brief, crooked smiles. Then she abruptly stepped forward and helped me to unclip my helmet and lift it off. I could instantly tell that Max had lowered the thermostat substantially, no doubt as an initial power-saving measure.

'How was it?' she asked.

'Oh, not too bad. Wind is picking up. I was starting to get blown around quite a bit towards the end. We'll have to watch that. If it gets much worse it's going to mean tethering gear and crampons. Max has probably told you that we need to fix the transmitter.'

'Yes, he said that. I'll help if you want.'

'That would be great. We have the spare dish here in the workshop and I'll have to do a bit of rewiring. But I tested the connection and it's fine.'

Leila nodded and placed my helmet on the storage shelf while I climbed out of the rest of the suit.

'Any news about Tad?' I asked. She shook her head.

'I've stayed away so I don't know. I didn't find anything in the DNA tests either.'

'No?'

'Well I couldn't see any particular virus or bacteria that

would account for the fever.'

'Maybe it's neither.'

'You mean some sort of native methanogen?'

I nodded.

Leila shrugged. 'Tad and Konrad were certainly both working with samples from as far as the troposphere, trying to create cultures. But the reality is, we've been searching for the last two years for some sort of life on Titan – and come up with precisely nothing.'

'Maybe we're looking for the wrong thing.'

'Meaning?'

'I don't know. Remember that old movie 'Andromeda Strain'? A satellite brings down some sort of extraterrestrial microbe with neither RNA nor DNA. It doesn't even have any amino acids. Yet it still transforms matter into energy.'

'Well anything is possible. But here on Titan we know any such life form would almost certainly have to take in H_2 instead of O_2. And it would get energy by reacting that H_2 with acetylene instead of glucose, to produce methane instead of carbon dioxide. Just how would such an organism live within one of us?'

'I don't know. Maybe after a mutation?'

'A pretty long bow to draw, don't you think? Especially when we haven't the slightest evidence of anything like that existing. And when we're only talking about a twenty four hour fever.'

'I suppose you're right.'

'You watch too many videos,' said Leila with another broken smile. She pulled back her sleeve and extended a hand. 'Come on then. It's past lunch time and I'm hungry.'

Max walked into cafeteria just as we were finishing our meal.

'Ah Edin. How's the head?'

My palm's bandaging, which was starting to dry and curl, scratched the top of my ear as I instinctively reached for the lump. I could feel the firm line of the glue stitching, some clumping of the hair. 'It's okay.'

'Still taking the buprenorphine?'

'Ah... yes.' In fact, I had the box in my pocket. I'd already taken two that morning but I wasn't sure if I should tell him. I knew my sensation of walking on a cloud was chemical – at least partly.

'Remember to go easy on them. We can't exactly manufacture stuff like that out here. The poppies and hemp we're growing aren't the same thing, are they?' He grinned and slapped me on the back. 'Listen, Tad's been calling for you. I can't shut him up. Can you do us a favour and speak to him?'

'What does he want?'

'He won't say. For your ears only, it seems.'

I looked at Leila and she rolled her eyes.

'He's quite anxious. And I'd rather not just up the sedative, if for no other reason than rationing.'

'So he's not much better then,' I ventured.

Max breathed in deeply and said, on the exhalation: 'Not really. But it's early days.'

I was about to take my plate to the sink when I felt Leila's hand on mine.

'I'll take care of the dishes. Just go. Get it over with.'

'Hey there Tad. How are you feeling?'

I heard the door behind me click shut. Tad was sitting up in bed, still hooked up to the drip, looking off to the side. He gradually turned his head in my direction. When he didn't reply, I added: 'You look a lot better than when I last saw you, my friend!'

Tad finally said, his voice barely above a whisper: 'You've got to help me. You're the only one who can.'

'How can I help you? Just say the word and I'll do it.' I sat down on the edge of his bed. His hand suddenly shot out and grabbed my forearm in a grip so tight his knuckles whitened. He was digging his fingers into a nerve at the head of the muscle.

'Take it easy man. You're safe now. Everything is going to be okay,' I said, trying to loosen his grip gently. He held on resolutely.

'It's this place. It's killing me. It's killing you too. You've got to get us out of here. You know that, don't you?'

I gave up trying to extricate myself and just placed my hand over his, patting it firmly. 'Listen, you've taken a few knocks to the head. You're just confused. Everything is going to be fine. It'll just take a couple of days.' I was starting to wonder how the hell we were going to cope with Tad down in the greenhouse. For a brief moment I uncharitably thought that maybe it would have been better had he not made it through the night.

'You're getting it – right? It's you and me. We're the only ones left. We're just seeing things from different times. Different angles.'

'You have to calm down dude.' I started to panic a little and wrenched out of his grip.

'I want you,' Tad said, leaning forward off his cushion, 'to get us to the launch vehicle. We'll go together, just like we came here together.' He smelled of stale breath and hospital tape. I looked up and saw the blood pressure monitor start, the bag on his arm inflating.

'We didn't arrive together Tad. You came with Konrad and Leila.'

'You're not listening to me! This place... it's changing

me. It's changing us all. I can see it now.'

'Tad, we're safe…'

'It's like I've been possessed by something – a higher power. I see it so clearly. You, me, Issy…'

I stood up. 'What about Isabella?' Tad had met my wife years before, but only briefly.

'If I don't make it, I want you to tell her I'm sorry. For everything.'

'What the hell are you talking about Tad? You don't mean my wife, Isabella?'

'Yeah man, I do. I'm so sorry.'

'What the fuck Tad!' I stepped back angrily towards the door. 'I'm going to call Max now. You need help.' Tad collapsed back in his bed. Tears were welling in his eyes and he started thrashing his head from side to side.

'Please, please! Take me to the launch vehicle. We can get out of here. Away from this madness!'

'The only madness is the stuff you're saying.'

'Don't do this! Please, listen…'

I shut the door and walked away. I could hear his voice wailing indistinctly through the wall.

Mean

'Pass me the Phillips head, will you?'

I was crouching down next to the antenna dish, putting in the final weatherproof clasp over the wiring. Leila was standing behind me, silhouetted. I saw her reach into the toolkit hanging over her shoulder, her torch momentarily blinding me as she swung the beam past my eyes. Then she straightened and proffered the screwdriver. For a brief moment I could see her face through the visor, a small fog near her mouth condensing and disappearing almost in the same instant, her dark eyes wide. Like me, she was fighting the stiff breeze. We were tethered together and to a large water-ice rock, our crampons squeaking as they dug into the surface.

'You never did say what happened when you went to see Tad,' she said. 'You've gone all quiet on me. That's not like you.'

Each of the screws had resisted me and the last one was being a particular nuisance. It was about half way in and the lost skin on my palm was stinging in protest at my efforts. I wished I had brought the electric drill. I was pretty sure the dressing on my palm had come off completely – the gloves of the suit kept pushing the pad around. I paused and turned around, a bead of sweat trickling down my nose. 'And how would you know what I'm like?'

Leila's silhouette didn't respond and I instantly regretted both my words and my tone. Not knowing what else to say, I resumed my work.

'That was uncalled for,' she replied eventually.

'I'm sorry. I'm upset. I shouldn't be taking it out on you.'

Leila remained silent for a while longer. 'Obviously it didn't go too well then.'

'Let's just say I'm starting to see why you don't like talking about him.' I grimaced in pain as I did a few more quarter turns. 'Was he like that while you were together?'

'Like what?'

'Stark raving mad.'

'You're being insulting again.'

'Sorry. Still venting.'

'You've got a mean streak, you know that? To answer your question, no. He started to change gradually.'

'How?'

'He got more and more clingy. Moody. Self-absorbed. I let him suck me in. I suppose I felt sorry for him. Eventually I realised he was drawing the life out of me.'

'Yeah, well I got a small dose of that today.'

A gust of wind threw my head back and I felt the line tighten as Leila lost her footing and swung up like a flag on a pole. She pulled herself back and dug in again. 'You know,' she said breathing hard, 'you're going to end up telling me what happened sooner or later.'

'You're probably right. For now, let's just say Tad's gone totally mental. I don't know how we're going to be able to tolerate him in the greenhouse. He'll drive us all nuts.'

'What else can we do?'

'I don't know. Push him out through the airlock?'

'Edin! I can't believe you said that!'

'Sorry.'

'What's got into you?'

'I don't know. He got under my skin, I guess.'

'How? For God's sake tell me.'

'He started talking about my wife.'

'In what way?'

'I don't know exactly. He implied they had some sort of history. Which is bullshit. As far as I know they only met once.'

Abruptly Leila started laughing. I watched her and quietly fumed. She was still chuckling as she said: 'Jesus, you can't be suspicious and jealous of something like that. Not from a distance of 1.2 billion kilometres. Not with all the time that's passed – and has yet to pass. And especially not with what's going on here.'

'What is going on here?'

'Don't play stupid. You know perfectly well. In fact, I'm sure that's why you didn't want to talk about it. You didn't want to break the cardinal rule.'

'Which is?'

'Never mention spouses. They aren't meant to exist.'

I decided not respond to that and finished the last few quarter turns with the screwdriver, grunting as I did so. Then I straightened and faced her. She was swaying gently on the rope, leaning with her back into the wind. 'I'm not suspicious. Or jealous,' I said. 'It just pissed me off – along with the other crap he was saying.'

'And that 'other crap' was…?'

'Oh, I don't know. He was insisting that he and I should take the launch vehicle and head home.'

'What? Just the two of you?'

'Yep. Just the two of us.'

'Sounds romantic. What were the rest of us meant to do?'

I snorted, picked up the old dish and hurled it up as I high as I could. We tracked it with our torch beams as the wind carried it away into the inky blackness. 'I don't know. He seemed to think the rest of you didn't even exist. Like the spouses back home, I suppose.'

Talk about the weather

The trip back home should have taken ten minutes. Instead it took just short of an hour and a half.

The wind picked up so much that we were forced to move from marker to marker: an agonizing process of tethering to one rock, reaching for the next, tethering to that, releasing the earlier tether, then doing it all again. At least we knew that by following the painted markers, we were unlikely to get lost – unless of course a rope failed, in which case we might be blown miles off course – maybe hundreds of them.

As it was, we were constantly being swept off our feet. There were times both of us simply hung on our tethers, swinging in the wind until it died down enough to inch forward again. I recall thinking that it felt like swimming against a rip. We became so exhausted that even in the low gravity we could barely lift an arm or a leg.

Unsurprisingly we didn't speak at all for the last hour, other than to answer Max's regular ten minute radio checks. In the long periods of silence both Leila and I became lost in our own worlds – worlds comprising something other than the buffeting, deafening wind and the utter blackness surrounding our narrow beams of torch light.

I actually think I lapsed into an alpha-wave brain state: I seemed to be dreaming even while stretching for a rock or clinging helplessly to the rope.

For me, the whole experience was reminiscent of hibernation while travelling to and from Earth. The ship's computer puts you in a hypothermia-induced torpor: one where your body's metabolism is slowed to a virtual standstill. Some people remember practically nothing when they wake up. Others, like me, can recall countless vivid dreams. But whichever way it goes, the hibernation seems timeless. It feels like you're lying down one moment and getting up the next.

Dreams become 'extra' memories that are 'outside of your time line': they don't correspond to any order or tense. A million things might seem to happen, but you won't be able to remember exactly when. It's almost as if time stops – but somehow you continue.

That's how it felt that night.

When we finally crawled in behind the perimeter wall, we both collapsed and lay there in the 'yard' outside the glowing greenhouse, next to a giant piece of insulation foam from the substation. I recall feeling bitterly cold, even though I was sweating inside my suit. Leila must have felt the same because she crawled into my arms and we lay there in the squeaky dust, instinctively (but pointlessly) hugging for warmth and dozing.

I awoke to our suits' alarms – we were running out of oxygen. I could hear and feel Leila's buzz first and mine a moment later. I groggily roused myself to a sitting position. At the same time Max called again on the radio.

'Edin, Leila. This is Max. Do you copy, over.'

'We're here Max. In the yard.'

'Where? Ah – I see you. I'm in the greenhouse. Of all the stupid places to lie down! Get the hell inside you two – you'll be running out of oxygen soon.'

'I know. Just had to recuperate a bit. Coming now.'

'Do you need any medical assistance?'

'Nah, we're fine. Just exhausted.'

'You sure?'

'Yeah, yeah. You try fighting those winds… It's insane out there.'

'Well, we have a satellite link again, so you've saved the day. Well done. Now get yourselves inside – that's an order! I'll be here setting up our new temporary habitat. Call me on my pager if you need anything. Sandra's bringing the last of the supplies down from the infirmary. You can help me with Tad a bit later – we'll bring him last. By hook or by crook, we've got to power down the upper levels by 20:00.'

I looked down at Leila but she was still asleep. Both her suit and mine started to buzz intermittently – one starting just after the other, like two toasters popping up in succession – indicating the final warnings: the levels of oxygen were getting dangerously low. Leila however stayed dead to the world.

'Leila. We've got to get inside,' I said gently. 'Leila, wake up honey.'

'Hmm?' She stirred. The visor was fogging with her slow, deep breaths. By the light of the greenhouse I could see her glassy eyes. I pulled her up into a seated position.

'Come on – let me help you.'

I ended up carrying Leila into the airlock. After that I let her stumble towards the bench and she flopped down onto it. I removed our helmets and started peeling her out of her suit. But as I did so, I noticed she was shivering uncontrollably. Her lips in particular trembled and she was making a vibrating sound between them. I decided to refasten her suit.

'It's cold,' she said, staring into middle distance.

'I know – I feel it too. Max must have lowered the thermostat some more. Don't worry – I'll get you warm soon.'

I wondered whether to take her straight to Max. But the greenhouse was bound to be even colder – its insulation was nowhere near as good as the rest of the base. Then it occurred to me that the warm interior of the glider would be ideal. So I picked her up in my arms and headed for the hangar.

Locked out

I had Leila lying across the rear seats, her back up against the curved fuselage.

'So cold,' she said, her voice wavering.

'Not long now,' I replied turning up the thermostat even more. I twisted around in the pilot's seat watching her and listening to the hum of the fan. Max wouldn't be happy about the battery use, but I didn't think it could be helped. I'd tell him later.

'You know when we were out there?' Leila said with her eyes closed.

'Yeah?'

'I started to see things.'

'Me too. Just like in hibernation.'

'Nuh, uh.' She shook her head slowly like a drunk. 'Not me. I never dream when they put me under.'

'You probably do. You just don't remember. It's the propofol. It makes most people forget. Amnesiac effect, they call it.'

'It made me think,' Leila said, her eyes opening just a fraction, 'about what you said before.'

'What did I say?'

'That stuff about methanogens.' She stumbled on the last word.

'We weren't breathing the atmosphere Leila.'

'I know.' Her voice was slurred. 'Obviously. But maybe

we've been exposed to it all along. Maybe some of it gets through. Like the hydrogen cyanide.'

'I doubt it. Anyway, we were hallucinating because of sensory deprivation and hypothermia.' I looked at the thermostat. It had climbed to twenty degrees Celsius. Leila was still shaking like someone with Parkinson's.

'Nope. I think it has to do with something out there.' Leila closed her eyes again. 'Still so cold.'

'You should be warming up by now.'

'I'm not. Turn it up please.'

But I was starting to sweat. I noticed Leila's cheeks were flushed. So I climbed over the seats, grabbed the first aid kit, pulled out the thermometer and pressed it into her ear.

Forty point five degrees Celsius.

'I'm still half in that twilight world. You know? Seeing things. Time is all messed up. So confusing.'

'No wonder Leila,' I said, checking again. This time it was forty point nine. 'You're burning up.'

'Ah.' She raised an arm weakly. 'I told you. It's in the air we breathe.'

'Yes, I'm afraid you've got that twenty four hour virus.'

'The one we can't detect.'

'The very same. I'll get Max. Hold on.' I slipped an arm outside of my suit, unclipped my pager and keyed in Max's code. I let it buzz half a dozen times, then gave up. 'He must have put his pager down.'

'Geez I feel awful,' she said, curling up into a ball.

I bent down and grabbed the box of paracetamol out of the first aid kit. But when I opened it I found the blister packets were all empty. The same thing happened with the ibuprofen. Either Tad or Konrad had been using the medicines without bothering to replace them.

As I was closing the kit I saw Tad's transceiver on the

cabin floor, partially under the pilot seat. The light showed it was on. I picked it up and pressed the call button – 'Max, are you there?' White noise greeted me. I tried a couple of times more before giving up and plugging the transceiver back into the console where it should have been. 'That's strange. It seems Tad's radio was working the whole time. I wonder why he never answered us?'

Leila, who was now hugging her knees and rocking herself, didn't respond. I noticed her breathing was getting ragged. I put my hand on her cheek, felt the heat radiating like an oven.

'I'm going up to the infirmary,' I said slipping my arm into my suit. 'Don't worry, I'll be back soon.' She merely nodded.

I bounded up the stairs all the way to the top level, keyed the pad to open the hermetic seal and pulled. The door stuck fast. I tried again and got the same result. Had they already sealed the level? I used my pager to call Sandra. She wasn't answering either but this time I let it keep buzzing. She might be carrying something with Max, after all. Eventually I heard the beep announcing a connection.

'Sandy? I can't open the door to the level three. Are you in there?'

Silence.

'Sandy, can you hear me?' I lowered the pager and checked to see if it was working. The readout displayed: 'Connected – Sandra Bruckner'. I tapped it a few times. 'Sandy, are you there? Please answer.'

'Sandra can't speak with you right now.'

It took me a moment to recognise the voice.

'Tad?'

More silence.

'Tad, I need to get up to the infirmary. It's urgent. Are

you all in the greenhouse?'

'No. Not in the greenhouse. Max is down there.'

'Where are you?'

'Sandra and I are here. On level three.'

'Okay, so put her on.'

'I can't.'

'Why not?'

Silence.

'What's happened Tad?'

'I can't tell you.'

'Why not? You're not making any sense.'

'She just can't speak with you right now.'

'Well at least open the door then. Are you able to move around?'

'Yes, I unplugged myself. Just pulled the drip out. I made a bit of mess.'

'Don't worry about that. Listen, can you get to the control room?'

'Yes, I can.'

'Okay. Go to the console. Find the security override for level three and press it.'

'I don't want to do that.'

'Why the fuck not?'

'Because I only just locked the doors.'

'You locked the doors? Why?'

'Because when I came downstairs I couldn't find you and Leila.'

'You were downstairs? When?'

'About ten minutes ago. I found Max but not you guys.'

'Tad, what the hell are you playing at? Just open the door for fuck's sake!'

'I don't want to talk any more. I have to go now.'

'Hold on! Tad!'

The connection terminated.

I leaped down the steps, and hurled myself along the tunnel to the greenhouse, bouncing off the walls. I was running so fast I couldn't stop myself crashing into the door with my shoulder. I keyed the pad frantically, pulled on the handle and thankfully it opened.

'Max!' I heard my voice resonating in the ghostly glow. I could see a table with five chairs. Next to it were stacked boxes of freeze dried food, kitchen equipment, medical supplies and our locally made paper for toilet use. Three thin double mattresses had been laid out in a row on the ground. 'Max!'

I started running between the hydroponic rows, the pulse pounding in my temples. But Max was nowhere to be seen. Had he gone outside? That was it! When we went to the glider he must have gone looking for us! But why hadn't he called us on our pagers? Or tried the radio? We would have heard him on Tad's transceiver.

I started running to the edge of the dome to look out into the yard when I tripped on something. I did a full somersault and landed on my back, sliding feet-first into one of the hydroponic containers which was knocked over in a slow shower of water and plant material.

That's when I found him. I turned around to see what had tripped me up and saw his shoe sticking out from under a tray table. I picked myself up, walked over and reluctantly lifted the tray. Max was lying in a pool of blood, his eyes wide open, a scalpel thrust deep into his trachea.

Then I felt a hard rush of wind and my ears popping. Tad was letting out the habitat's air.

The world where you live

I knew instantly what was happening, yet it still took me a moment to react.

I was still standing there over Max's body wondering whether to administer CPR when the wind started to whistle past me. I looked up to see that the door to the tunnel had been flung wide open. Tad was almost certainly doing that to all the exits. He'd probably disabled the hermetic seals so that even if I tried to close a door, the air would still seep out – and Titan's frozen, reactive atmosphere would then start to seep in. So I dropped the tray I was holding and started running, the wind at my back.

By the time I entered the tunnel, the doors at both ends were banging.

I was running so fast that I practically flew into the workshop and was forced to turn my back to the approaching wall and brace for the collision. I gasped on impact, felt my ribcage being compressed, my kidneys being crushed. A fraction of a second later my head whip-lashed against the wall's plastic outer shell and I felt my newly knitted scar reopen – a flush of hot blood in the rapidly cooling air. Then I slid down to the ground, my feet slipping out from under me as I struggled to gain a grip on the floor.

Leila's and my helmets were still on the shelf. I grabbed

one in each hand and ran towards the hangar, the door to which was also flapping in the wind. I went to slip through as it was opening, but my timing was off and the edge caught me across the back and shoulder muscles, causing me to drop one of the helmets. I watched it bounce towards the blackness outside and sprawled into the hangar after it as the door snapped open again.

When I tried to breathe, the cold seemed to squeeze my lungs like a sponge being wrung-out. What little air I did manage to heave in burned my trachea like green-leaf smoke.

Luckily the helmet collided with the fuselage of the glider and I caught it against my chest on the rebound. I pulled at the canopy hatch with my free hand, felt the warm air blast me in the face, threw the helmets and then myself inside, and pulled the canopy shut.

The cacophony ceased.

Leila was lying across the back seats, her chest heaving as she tried to breathe. I heard the glider's internal fans working overtime to restore the air pressure.

I knew I had little time, so I climbed into the pilot's seat, engaged the engine and pushed the reverse button. The glider started to back out slowly.

Too slowly.

Leila started coughing – a dry, spasmodic cough – then vomited, the sweet, acidic stench reaching my nostrils almost before the air from the fans blasting in my face. A bubble floated and splattered onto the dash.

'What's happening,' she managed.

'It's Tad. He's opened all the exits. He's trying to drop the air pressure.'

'Looks like he's succeeding,' said Leila pointing to the monitor. Outside I could see the wind dying down as the pressure in the habitat equalised with the exterior.

'Uh oh. We've got a few minutes at most to get the hell out of here.'

I was looking at my rear monitor when I heard the grinding of the hangar door. On screen I saw it starting to lower.

'The bastard's seen us. He's trying to shut us in.'

Leila crawled into the front seat, grabbed the remote and pressed it frantically. The door stopped with a shudder. The glider was still patiently inching its way out. 'Can't this thing go any faster?'

'Afraid not – this is the maximum reverse speed. It isn't really designed to go backwards in a hurry. Buckle up,' I said, clipping myself into my harness. Leila adjusted herself into her seat and did the same.

Suddenly the grinding noise resumed.

'Damn! He's overridden our remote!'

Leila, who was still frantically pushing on it with both thumbs, yelled: 'Hurry!'

'I'm doing everything I can!'

A loud screeching filled the cabin as the top of the glider caught the door just above the cockpit.

For a moment we lurched to a halt, the glider's small reverse engine humming. I smelled burning. Then we abruptly broke loose, the hangar door scraping down the plexiglass windscreen, taking wide gouges out of the plastic. It gave us a final shuddering slap across the nose as we cleared the entrance.

Just before the door closed, I saw the lights inside the hangar flicker and switch off.

I taxied backwards to the clear space on the left, straightened up and put the glider into forward gear.

That's when we remembered the perimeter wall was still up.

'What the hell do we do?' asked Leila.

'Hang on,' I said, turning towards the greenhouse. 'The yard is about as long as the runway. If we can build up enough speed, we should clear the wall.'

I manoeuvred past some debris, drew parallel to the habitat and pulled back the throttle. We heard the whine as the glider picked up speed. The greenhouse on our right, lit like a Christmas tree, started to blink out. The last light went off as we became airborne. A moment later we cleared the perimeter wall by less than a metre.

We were a few hundred metres up when we heard a dull rumble. Then came the explosion that flung us upwards like a rag doll, spinning into the darkness.

The explosion threw us many kilometres off course and high up into the atmosphere, but I managed to track back down using the launch vehicle's homing beacon and the infra-red cameras. Leila vomited twice more filling the cabin with muck and stench, but after that she settled.

The presence of the beacon was comforting – it showed that the launch vehicle was intact. But then again, that's exactly why it had been placed on the other side of the hill from the habitat and substation. I circled, setting down to a low speed at an altitude of about twenty metres so that the glider's lights gave some indication of the terrain – any lower and the off-ground turbulence made for an unstable ride.

When I thought I was as close as I was likely to get, I turned into the headwind to reduce the speed and brought it down to land on the west side which we'd worked hard to clear as a general landing area. Because of the pitch darkness I fully expected the glider to hit a rock or maybe some debris and overturn, but somehow we got lucky.

The homing beacon said we were within fifty metres of the launch vehicle, but we stayed in the glider's cockpit for another half an hour waiting for the winds to die down.

Eventually a slight lull made me rouse Leila who had been sleeping in the copilot seat. We donned our helmets, switched on our suits, opened the canopy to a rush of escaping air, then followed the direction of the beacon as indicated by the radio. Other than our clothes and suits, this would be the only thing we would take from this world in which we had lived.

We weren't tethered except to each other, so I was feeling a mild sense of panic when, after several minutes, we still couldn't find the launch vehicle. My trepidation was made worse by the fact that our suits were now buzzing more or less continuously, warning of imminent oxygen depletion.

Abruptly it became clear that we had overshot: we were now walking across a field strewn with large boulders. So we back-tracked in the pitch darkness, tripping and stumbling and fighting the cross-winds until we were on cleared ground once more. The battery in the radio died just as we saw the launch vehicle materialise out of the gloom, its dark outline illuminated by our headlight torches.

I powered up the auxiliary system and left it to run another full diagnostic while I helped Leila up the rungs to the airlock.

Once inside, I strapped her into her seat, found the medical kit and forced her to take two paracetamol and two ibuprofen tablets.

Then I powered up the thrusters, set the program to orbit, strapped into my own seat and pressed ignition.

The sudden acceleration gave me a rush of nausea. I

was also starting to feel cold. In fact, by the time I could see the glowing crescent of Titan's atmosphere I was shivering uncontrollably.

Dreaming

We were in orbit and I was configuring the return journey. The next scheduled launch window was still a year away but our hydrocarbon processing on Titan meant we had more than enough fuel to boost the velocity and make up the difference if the need ever arose.

I'd recorded a short video report and sent it home, advising of an atmospheric breach at the base and loss of all but two lives.

It takes an hour and twenty four minutes for a signal to be received and the same for a reply. But I wasn't going to wait for that – the computer had calibrated the adjustments and we were ready to go. Besides, I was feeling increasingly groggy and unwell. The pounding in my head, constant shivering and a sense of nausea were interfering with my thoughts. As it was, the message I'd recorded and sent probably didn't make much sense. Hopefully they would have seen the blood on my scalp and understood that I wasn't really fit to talk.

I turned to Leila who appeared to be sleeping. I'd already helped her to get strapped into her hibernation chamber.

'You awake?'

She mumbled: 'Mm. Not really. Not asleep either. That in-between world.'

'Symptoms any better?'

'About the same. Do you still have some of Max's tablets?' She was speaking with her eyes closed.

I felt in my pocket and was surprised to find the box still there: a bit flattened but intact. I was about to take a wafer out when I realised it might be contraindicated for those about to undergo hibernation, so I said: 'Afraid not. Must have left them at the base.'

'Damn. You were always hogging them.' She frowned, shook her head and breathed out a long sigh.

'Don't worry – I'll be giving you something better very soon when I put you under.'

I floated to the console to program the hibernation chambers. Once strapped in, you had to connect yourself to monitors, put on an oxygen mask and insert a cannula which was programmed to release a sustained combination of fentanyl, propofol and midazolam to keep you under. The lid then shut and the chamber cooled you to just under four degrees Celsius. Hydrogen sulfide was used to stabilise your body's core temperature in the hypothermic environment.

Leila abruptly said: 'I've been thinking about the whole issue of time. How we can't see it for what it really is.'

'Uh huh.' She was starting to ramble again.

'I'm thinking maybe we can still see it through a kind of prism. Except your brain doesn't know how to interpret things and this distorts your perception. Changes things around. Messes with the order. Messes with perspectives.'

'I get the feeling I'll know what you mean in a little while.'

'How's that?'

'I've come down with that fever of yours.'

'Of mine?' She raised her voice but still didn't open her eyes. 'Since when was it mine?'

'Just a figure of speech.'

'So sorry to make you sick. Take some paracetamol.'

'I already have.'

I could see a frown etched on her forehead.

'We'll get over it soon enough,' I said. 'It'll probably pass during the first few hours of hibernation. Speaking of which, I'm starting the prep. I'll do you first.' I put on her monitoring pads and started to roll up her sleeve to insert the cannula.

'You've 'done' me already.' She opened her eyes. I noticed they were bloodshot.

'Come again?'

'You've 'done' everybody – haven't you?'

'Leila, I really don't know what you're on about.'

'I'm thinking of how cruel you are.'

'And I'm thinking your fever is doing the talking,' I said, finding the vein. Leila didn't resist.

'Go fuck yourself.' I felt bubbles of her spittle hit me in the face. Her breath still smelled of vomit. 'I spoke with Sandra. She told me how you treated Tad. The things you said about him.'

'What did I say?' I'd got the vein. I taped the cannula in and I pressed the button for the saline solution.

'Same stuff you told me: how he was losing it. That he needed to be pushed out of the airlock.'

'I never said anything like that.'

Leila laughed. 'You've forgotten already? How convenient.'

'That was me speaking with you. I was angry. I never said anything like that to Sandra.'

'Do you know how she must have felt hearing someone say that about her own brother?'

'Brother? I'm afraid you're totally confused. Look, I'm going to put you under now.'

'And the base,' she added, grabbing me by the arm. 'Did you have to destroy it? It's not good enough that you killed your crew. You had to come into our little world and wreck that too.'

'My crew died when their hibernation chambers malfunctioned. That's been logged.'

'Bullshit. Where were the bodies? Tell me – what happened to their bodies? What did you do with Tad and Konrad?'

I wanted to tell her exactly what had happened to the bodies – but strangely I could no longer remember. Instead I said: 'You know very well that I didn't do anything with them.'

'You killed them and pushed them out of the airlock. Then you blamed it on a malfunction.'

'Are you suggesting I came here with Tad and Konrad? That they were my crew?' I shook my head and carried on working with my free hand. At the same time it dawned on me that I couldn't remember my crew members. Neither their names, nor even their faces.

Leila snorted in response and released her grip. 'Go on. Put me to sleep. God knows what it will really do.'

'It's going to put you in hibernation. I'm giving you fentanyl now.'

'And this little thing?' she tapped her stomach. 'What happens to our baby?'

I paused and stared at her. She glared back. In the end I said: 'Leila, you're delirious. I'm going to start the propofol and midazolam. I'll see you on the other side.'

'You don't even care, do you? And you never cared about me. Hitting on what's her name like I simply didn't exist. Notice how you held onto the box of ondansetron Max gave me? You didn't give a shit that I needed it for morning sickness. You've seen me vomiting. I bet you still have it in your pocket. I'm right – aren't I?' She pointed to the square outline of the box of buprenorphine visible on my pants.

'Goodnight Leila.' I pressed the button and she slumped almost instantly. I pulled the oxygen mask over her face and pushed away from her chamber, watching the lid closing automatically. Within seconds the glass clouded over.

Inserting your own cannula isn't easy. I decided to do it first, before strapping myself in and putting on the monitors. I made a total mess of it on the back of my left hand, then tried my forearm, then swapped to the right side. Finally I managed to find a vein after bruising myself horribly.

It didn't help that my hands were shaking. Part of it was the fever. Obviously the other part was my final interaction with Leila. I consoled myself that I would soon be falling into a blissful sleep and none of it would matter.

I strapped myself into the chamber, and started placing the monitor pads on myself. The box of buprenorphine had however twisted in my pocket and was digging into my thigh, so I undid everything, sat up and pulled it out. I had already released the box to float about the cabin when something made me grab it back and examine it.

The label said 'Ondansetron'.

I broke into a sweat, pushed myself away from the hibernation chamber and made my way to Leila's. I rubbed at the glass for a moment until I realised the futility, then bent down to look through a gap in the fog. I saw Isabella.

That's when I went back, strapped myself in, connected the pads and cannula, pulled the mask over my face and pressed the panel buttons.

The last thing I remember is the lid closing as I fell backwards into a hazy shade of twilight.

Shadows

I woke to find that Konrad was already up: his bunk was empty. Tad no longer slept in his – he stayed in front of the video monitor watching old movies in endless succession till exhaustion took him and he slept. Then he woke and watched again.

Neither helped with the logs and maintenance protocols. And neither bothered with the set exercises.

I floated through the narrow passage, fingers brushing the puny hull. Through the porthole I could see a billion stars – cold, unblinking points of light on a black velvet canvas. There was no Sun, no Moon.

As I squeezed into the control room Konrad was pushing food into his mouth. Tad was in front of the monitor watching a Western, talking softly to himself in an unintelligible dribble – the volume on the video was muted. Konrad looked up, sneered, then went back to his food.

Tad shrieked unexpectedly: 'My God they're coming!' He held his hands up to shield himself from the monitor. 'Someone please stop them!'

Konrad suddenly hurled his dessert at Tad's back – food splattered into a thousand bubbles that dispersed in the cabin. 'Shut up, you fucking loony!' Tad moaned and cowered into a ball. 'What's your problem Edin? Go do your fucking logs.' Konrad reached for another dessert.

'Konrad, that food has to be rationed…'

Tad shrieked again: 'Stop them! Can't you see? Please – oh please!'

Konrad's jaw tightened and he closed his eyes. 'I told you to SHUT THE FUCK UP!'

Tad covered his eyes and screamed – on screen the Indians charged.

'He needs help. I don't think he's eaten in days…'

'Good – maybe he'll die sooner.'

'Look, we need to get through this together.'

Konrad replied in a mocking falsetto: 'Get through this? How? Shall we try the transmitter again? Can't you get it through your thick skull that it's no use? Look! LOOK!' He grabbed me with both hands by the scruff of my overalls and jostled me toward the porthole. I struggled free and we collided with the cabin wall. 'There isn't anything out there for a billion miles! Get it? There's nothing – just you, me and the loony! Nothing else exists!'

For a few moments we watched each other in the hum of silence. The room narrowed in my eyes. Somewhere in the distance Tad whimpered and babbled, a red warning signal had begun to flash and an alarm was sounding. Konrad pushed himself back into the centre of the cabin where his dessert was suspended. It was only then that the urgency of the situation dawned on me.

'That's a radiation alert – you've got to help me with Tad!' But Konrad was going back to his bunk, clutching the dessert to his chest. 'Konrad! KONRAD!'

I floated over to Tad who was mumbling as he held his head in his hands, rocking from side to side.

'I knew they would come, I just knew it. But no one would listen.'

I grabbed his arm above the smeared food and tried to pull him towards the floor hatch of the Safe Room, but

Tad shrugged away.

'Don't touch me! GET AWAY!'

'Look, it's just me, Edin, okay? I want to help.'

'You! I know you! Get away from me!' Tad recoiled, flailing his arms wildly, eyes wide. I tackled him around his thin shoulders and we crashed against the hull where he initially struggled then became limp, lapsing into a sobbing fit. Then I started towing him, the alarm shrieking in the background. By the time we reached the hatch any semblance of fight had deserted him: Tad had been reduced to a quivering man-child, racked by sobs and smeared with food, tears and snot.

The 'Safe Room' was more like cupboard. Inside, we waited in the dim light, watching the flashing indicator. I cradled Tad in my arms until his crying faded to hiccupping sniffs and deep sighs. A photograph was taped to the thick insulation. It was the three of us at the launch pad, smiling and confident.

Then the flashing stopped, the signal glowed amber and after a while it turned green. I moved Tad aside to find he was asleep.

When I opened the hatch I almost immediately sensed something was different – the slight 'pop' in my ears, a strangeness in the air.

Konrad!

I groped my way into the passage, missing the hand rails, crashing against the sides. After I reached Konrad's bunk, I struggled frantically with the zipper. But the bunk was empty, save for the unopened dessert which floated absurdly against the padding and the velcro straps. I knew there was nowhere else to look.

At the porthole I was greeted by vacuum and frozen starlight.

A sudden wail cut through the silence like a razor. I

fumbled my way back to the cabin to see Tad hanging in the middle, ashen-faced and wide-eyed. When he spoke, his voice was dry and harsh.

'They're here.'

I came closer. 'Who's here?'

Tad began to moan, his voice slowly building to a crescendo. Then he clawed towards me, burrowing into my chest and looking over his shoulder. The sudden movement drove us into a corner.

Tad was screaming: 'Get away! GET AWAY!'

I scanned the cabin as I stroked Tad's matted hair. Abruptly, I shouted into the emptiness, although I didn't know why. Perhaps it was because of the chill that I felt at the back of my neck, perhaps it is because there was nothing else left to do. I could hear my voice yelling at the invisible pursuers: 'LEAVE ME ALONE!'

It took a while to realize that I was now in a different place altogether: a blank, featureless room of cold white. Tad was gone. I tried desperately to discern any detail, any form. But the room was empty save for the bleached glare. There were no shapes, no corners, no lines. No shadows.

Barcelona

When I woke again, it was a sudden, involuntary action –
like being startled out of a luxurious daydream. Except
there was no recognition, no sense of reconnection.
Instead I found myself lying on an incline in a white
hospital bed, arrested by crisp sheets, wondering what my
last thought had been. There was no explanation from the
throbbing ward which indifferently pursued its routine.
Across the aisle I could see a nurse measuring the blood
pressure of a patient who periodically grimaced. A partly
drawn curtain to my right revealed a withered, melanoma
crusted hand that twitched with the soft moans of its
owner. And to my left an open corridor stammered with
nondescript chatter and the clatter of hard soled shoes on
polished linoleum. Ordinary, unhurried activity, that was
oblivious to my disorientation. There was nothing to
which I could fix my memory, no sense of immediate past,
no explication of my environment: just an alien 'here and
now'.

In between the bleached sheets and musty-sweet smell
of stale skin and ammonia, the certainty of my confusion
began to crystallise. My reaction was infantile – like a cry
from a darkened crib – a voice I barely recognised that
croaked unexpectedly, then wailed. I had no idea to whom
I was crying – the nurse I suppose. He let the stethoscope
drop from his ears while his dark patient stirred.

Instead of coming to me, he called out into the corridor. It was a while before I realised he was not speaking in English but in melodic Latin tones that rose above the hum outside.

Almost at once, concerned, chatty figures began to fill the room. I heard more approaching footsteps in the corridor. Soon a crowd had gathered around me.

After some initial discussion the bulk of the onlookers departed, leaving only two: an older moustachioed man who sat next to me on the bed and a bronze-haired woman who drew the curtain across. I was still crying out and the man placed his hand on my mine.

'It's okay – you'll be okay – just take it easy Edin.'

'Where am I? What's going on? Please... please tell me what's happened.'

'You've had a close call mate, but you should pull through from here.' He patted my hand and the woman nodded. They were both dressed in scrubs.

'What the hell happened?'

'Don't you remember?' asked the woman. At that moment a group pushing a stretcher moved through the corridor and a man shouted out in an expressive barrage that faded as they moved down the hall.

'You were in a fight, Edin,' the man said, lowering his voice, 'you know – in the bar? The other fellow stabbed you in the head. You lost a lot of blood but you should be okay.'

I stared at him. 'What? What do you mean? What bar? Where the hell am I?'

'You're in the hospital – you've had to have surgery,' the woman answered.

'Which hospital?'

'Barcelona's general hospital, of course,' said the man.

'What the...? Barcelona?' I struggled and failed to find

some reference in my memory that would help me understand what he was saying. 'But how did I get here? Who are you?'

'Take it easy mate. We're fellow Aussies. Sandra here's from Sydney, I'm from Melbourne. When the emergency team saw your passport they called on us. That's as much as we know.' I read a plastic name tag on his shirt that proclaimed 'Max' in broad, felt tip pen. Sandra came closer to me and bent over slightly.

'Can you remember anything at all?'

'Yes, but... I can't remember... I... I've never... I don't remember coming here.'

'Do you know your name?'

'Markovic... Edin. I live in Perth. I've never even been overseas. How could this happen?' They could only frown in sympathy.

'Edin, do you know what year it is?' Sandra asked.

'I... I can't be sure.' I wanted to writhe out of the sheets that strapped me in but they conspired with my body to allow only a feeble movement in protest at my imprisonment. 'I just can't remember what happened last. It's... it's like a bad dream.' Max patted my hand again and stood up.

'You're suffering a partial amnesia – it's quite common after a trauma to the head. And apart from the stab wound it looks like you copped a beauty when you fell and smacked your head in the bar.'

'Bar? Damn it, I don't go to bars!'

Sandra walked around to where Max was standing and smiled. She said, 'It'll take a little while but it should all come back to you. In the meantime you should rest. One of us will come back a little later to conduct a full test and take some details. The police will also want to speak to you at some time – but don't think too much about that.'

'Yeah – try not to worry, mate. Everything will work out fine. We'll catch you later,' added Max.

And with that the Australians withdrew beyond the curtain where they spoke briefly to the nurse in Spanish, before disappearing down the hall.

I flopped my head back against the pillow and immediately felt the sting. I lifted my hand up to my head to examine the bandaging and found it surrounded by shaved stubble and dried blood that had caked like bark.

It was there, with my head back, that I noticed the landline on the bedside table to my left. I looked around for a mobile but couldn't remember whether I even had one. So I called out, "Nurse? Are you there?"

He abruptly pulled back the curtain. I saw his name badge read 'Chaz'.

'I'd like to use the telephone. Can I use the telephone?'

'I will be with you in a moment, please.' His English was heavily accented but I couldn't tell what kind.

'You speak English!'

'Yes.' He made some notes on his clipboard file, stashed it at the end of my bed and walked closer.

'I need to make a call to Australia…'

Chaz's brow furrowed.

'Please – you must help me!'

He abruptly shook his head, grabbed the phone and placed it on the bed. And then he was gone.

With trembling fingers, I began to dial '+61' and Issy's number. I waited, it seemed, an eternity for the line to connect and then another eternity while the phone rang. It occurred to me that he had no idea what time it was in Barcelona, never mind what time it would be in Perth. Finally I heard the connection and the sound of my wife's voice, as clear as if she were across town, except for the echo.

'Issy – Issy it's me, Edin.'

'What the … where –'

'Issy you've got to –'

'– blazes have you –'

'– help me – it's like a nightmare. Please, tell me what's happened.'

There was a silence on the other end as the echo finished repeating the message and then I heard my wife explode.

'You tell me! You've been missing for two years.'

Catching up

'Would you like to come back to my place and get dry? You can put your things near the heater.' Marta was looking up at him through the dark rings around her eyes. Konrad shifted a little so that his running shoes squelched and he laughed uncertainly.

'I was thinking of going to a tutorial in about five minutes, so maybe...'

'But you're all wet.'

Konrad laughed again. 'Well I suppose I'd feel a little uncomfortable in the tutorial. Are you sure, I mean...'

'No, it's all right. Mum's not even around. She's gone to visit my auntie in Melbourne.'

Konrad started to say something but faltered and shrugged, looking out into the fading light. The rain had slowed to a wispy veil, cast about by the breeze. Marta kept looking at him with a fixed expression.

'I might just take the bus home. It'll be okay, really.'

'You'll catch a cold. And it won't take long to get dry. Come on, it's just up the road.'

'Yes, I remember. Look it's really nice of you to offer but I wouldn't have anything to wear anyway, so I may as well stay wet until I get home.' Marta narrowed her eyebrows.

'You could just borrow an overcoat for a while, silly.'

'You sure? I really don't want to impose...'

Marta smiled. A drop of water ran down her cheek from a matted curl. 'Come on.' She beckoned him under her umbrella and they made their way across the carpark to the block of flats visible through the haze over the road from the university.

As Marta opened the deadlock to the apartment they were instantly enveloped by warmth and the dull smell of Brussels sprouts. She took off her coat and hung it up on a rack behind the door where she also placed her umbrella.

'Here, give me your jacket. Is it dry on the inside?'

'I'm afraid it's pretty much wet right the way through.'

'You poor thing.' Marta pulled it off his shoulders and walked down the wallpapered hallway into darkness.

'This is the same place you were in before?' he called out as a light flickered from a side door.

'Yes, of course. Come through.' He followed her voice around the corner to the brightness, his shoes squeaking. Marta was at the far end of a bedroom, hanging up the jacket next to a heater.

'It's nice and warm in here.'

'Yes. I've got the timer set so that it comes on before I'm home.' She turned and smiled. 'Why don't you have a hot shower? That'll warm you up. I'll hang the rest of your things next to the heater.'

'Marta, I really don't know... I shouldn't stay too long. Leila will be waiting. Do you remember Leila? I think you were introduced once. Years ago.'

'You're supposed to be at a tutorial aren't you? Anyway, you don't want to catch a cold.' She walked past him into the hallway and returned with a towel. 'Go on. Leave your clothes just outside the door. The bathroom is down the hallway on the left.'

'What about you...'

'I'm okay. I'm not nearly as wet as you are. Besides, I'll

wash up a bit at the basin and have a shower later. Really.'
She thrust the towel at him. He accepted it and took a step
backwards.

'Okay. Well, I suppose I'll just have a quick one then…'

Marta heard the bathroom door gently close as she
flipped through the hangers in the cupboard. She pulled
out a heavy overcoat which she held up to examine and
for a moment her eyes become distantly focused. She took
it into the hallway outside the bathroom where she called
through the closed door.

'There's an overcoat just outside.'

'Thanks Marta.'

'Grab it anytime, I won't look.'

'Oh, and uh…'

'Just leave your things outside as soon as you're ready.'

'That's great, thanks Marta.'

Konrad heard his voice boom in the chilly whiteness
of the bathroom and stared at the stack of salon
shampoos and conditioners, the floral shower caps,
smelled the soapy perfume. He peeled off his shirt and
struggled and tripped over his sodden jeans. When he was
finished he surveyed his body in the large mirror above
the basin, tensing his biceps and sucking in his stomach.

I blame myself for what happened. I was trying to get back
the past and anyone can tell you it isn't possible. I found
this out after I stopped being a lawyer and decided to
chase a stupid dream I couldn't define.

It was quite by chance that I was passing the university
after seeing a client and I thought I'd go in – to hell with
the old time-sheet counting my day in six minute intervals
and my usefulness to the firm, to hell with the 'let's see
who bills the most today' bullshit. I thought I'd just go
and hang out under the broad, sweeping figs, savouring

the shade and the cool breeze off the bay and the smell of warm pollen in amongst the sprinklers. I was hooked. Next thing I knew, I had told Leila I was going to leave my job – just for a year or two, mind you – and go back to uni. Back to when I was alive, not wrapping dead words in paper next to a stopwatch. Leila took it well in the circumstances. She said she'd support me – for a while anyway. I said I'd go back to psychology and finish my degree, that I wanted to learn about people and understand them.

Of course I didn't learn anything at all in the next few months. It was like being at work again: I started accepting every day for what it was, not expecting any great return to the glories of my memory. I tried to go to the tavern once or twice, but that was no good – just young kids getting hopelessly pissed and trying to be grown up. I seemed so much more sophisticated in my memories, so much better and wiser than they were. Of course I probably wasn't.

I learned my lesson later, mid-year. It was one of those days where the wind seems to howl up from the Antarctic and the rain blasts in right angles at you so you can't open your eyes enough to see. I was hanging around some kids who thought they were really cool and we were heading towards the ref. I had just about had enough of their posturing, their ignorance and their pathetic attempts at wit, so I said I'd pass things up and head for home.

'What about the five o'clock tute!' yelled this weedy, spoilt brat, little white pimples peering out amongst the ripening blackheads on his chin.

'I'll read up about it later', I called back through the gusting spray of the oval I was crossing to escape.

I was halfway across when the clouds really burst, like a dyke finally cracking and sweeping away the little boy plugging a hole with his finger. I tried to run, my bomber jacket pulled up around my neck. There was no shelter, no trees for a hundred metres. The water and the cold were invasive, thorough – like I was thrown in a pool of iced water. To make matters worse I was wading through puddles that were more like lakes and I could feel my toes going numb and shrivelling.

The rain had eased a bit when I saw her. She was hurrying along, her umbrella buffeting around like she was going to take off and parasail (she was small enough too). I instantly recognised her. She hadn't changed at all. Still hanging around the campus after all these years, still trying to fit into a world that didn't want her.

'Hey, Marta!' I called out and she stopped, mid-puddle, and looked at me with her wide-set eyes on her round face, a look of surprise or shock, I couldn't tell.

I could see that despite her umbrella she was almost as wet as I was. Her shoulder-length hair was plastered over her forehead and the raindrops hung like tears from her cheeks. She just stood there staring as I ran up and I wondered for a moment if she could even remember who I was. Then she smiled, her eyes narrowing into slits through the smeared mascara.

'Oh hi!' she said. As I ran up she offered her pathetic little umbrella and we headed, without saying anything else, for the engineering buildings on the far side of the oval. There, under the cover of the square, sixties' architecture and amongst the stale, blue-green mosaic we sheltered awkwardly next to each other, shaking rain and making disjointed small talk. 'It's so nice to see you! How have you been, you look the same as ever,' and so forth. She was vintage Marta, smiling sweetly, not saying much and making me strain to find things to say.

'I'm fine and how are you, Konrad?' she said looking

up with her head tilted and her eyes circled by the ridiculous mascara, or what was left of it.

'Good, good. I'm back at uni, did you know?' She shook her head and frowned in interest. 'Well I just had enough of work, you know the same old thing, day in and day out, so I thought I'd come back here and try something different.' She nodded at me and said nothing. 'I'm studying psychology. I have a few credits from before I did law.' Silence. 'What about you, still at the bank?'

'Actually, I'm at a different place now.'

'Oh, that's good. Same line of work?'

'It's another bank, but I'm in Customer Services.' She rubbed near her eye, looked at the blackness on her hand, then looked away. I stared out across the grey-streaked oval and said, 'Crazy weather, isn't it?'

'Yes.'

I don't know how we ever met. I think she was Tad's sister's friend from school. All I remember is that she started coming out with us to nightclubs and parties. Sweet Marta, the quiet girl of the group. Never said much, loved to dance and was good at it, her shapely bum meandering perfectly to the rhythm, the petite frame melting into the dance floor. Always a wide, embarrassed smile nestled between her bulbous cheeks. She was at her best on the dance floor or in bed, where her body did all the talking. I remember one particular night dancing up a storm in an old place called The Subway. It had the usual noisy, sweaty areas where people crammed themselves in, danced and screamed into each other's ears when they wanted to say something. There were also a few quiet bars and lounges – one in particular had a bloke playing an acoustic guitar in the corner. After getting too sweaty dancing I screamed in Marta's ear to come and have a drink, so we left the others and went down to that bar. I knew she liked me – she would always come and sit next to me when we invariably went to Tad's place after nightclubbing. Sometimes she would sit on my lap playfully and I would place my hands on her small waist and feel her trembling slightly.

On that particular occasion, I took her hand, feeling it hot and wet in my own, and lead her to the bar downstairs. But once we were there, seated in the comparative quiet and the privacy from the others, there just wasn't anything to say. Nothing. I liked her in lot of ways but it was as if there was a closed door between us. I might have fallen in love with her that night, I wanted to. It seemed so full of promise, of magic. I realised however in the dimmed light of the lounge, the soft chords of the solo guitarist wafting through the chilled air, that if it could not be perfect then, it never would be. That wasn't to say that we couldn't have fun together. We both loved to dance and I thought maybe it would be best if we could go back and do our talking up there. So after a few failed attempts at conversation, of wall watching awkwardness, I grabbed her hand again and led her back, making some comment about the lameness of the guitarist. I know that Marta felt it too: that we were not in our shared element, that we needed an equaliser. So she laughed with me and the atmosphere was restored.

When we were leaving the club that night my friends made the usual noises about going back to Tad's or to an all-night café. Marta was standing next to me, really close, and I could feel her moist warmth radiating into the coolness of the night. For some reason I didn't feel too much like an all-nighter so I said, 'I'll pass, I've had enough.'

'You sure Konrad?' Tad looked like he was trying to say something. I knew he was trying to make out with

Isabella, though it was early days yet and he wanted any excuse to spend more time with her.

'No, I'm sure Tad. You guys go on ahead. I'll call a taxi.'

'I'll give you a lift,' Marta said. I still remember the matter-of-factness in her voice though I saw for the briefest of instants a knowing look in her wide-set eyes under the yellow street lamp.

'Not you too! What a bunch of party poopers.' Tad shook his head, his brow knotted.

Looking back now, I realise that this evening marked the beginning of the end of my raging days. Things never seemed to be the same afterwards. To begin with I had exams and shortly thereafter I met Leila through, would you believe it, one of my father's colleagues. But that night Marta and I had fun as young people do – the heart-pumping, non-cerebral, experimental fun of youth.

Mum says there's no such thing as love, but I don't think that's true. I think she's sour because Dad left us. She's never really gotten over that. I don't remember Dad. It all happened when I was little so maybe that's why I'm not all twisted up. I know I was in love once, and that was with Konrad Gruber. I remember when I first saw him. He came to Sandra's place to see her brother. It was Saturday afternoon and I thought I'd go and see if Sandra was doing anything. I met Sandra when I worked as a receptionist at a clinic where she was a nurse. Her family lived in Shenton Park. Most people in the western suburbs are snobbish and stuck up. I know because I've lived in Nedlands since I was in high school. I said Sandra's family wasn't snobbish, but Tad (her brother) was just the worst. He was desperately wanted to be just like all the others.

We were talking with Tad, teasing him and so on, when this friend of his came in and I thought: 'This guy is cute!'

He was tall, with thick dark hair and grey eyes that made you feel like he had x-ray vision or something. Also, he smiled a lot. I was really shy back then so I didn't say anything, but Sandra was quite confident so she talked to him, mostly about uni. I was silly really. I never used to say anything because I was afraid people would think I was thick and laugh at me. Mum says: 'Rather have people think you're stupid, than open your mouth and remove all doubt.'

So that afternoon I was just listening to all that was going on and how they were going out to a party when suddenly the cute guy looks at me and Sandra and says: 'Are you coming along?'

'I didn't know we were invited,' says Sandra.

'Yes, of course you're invited. Hey Tad, it's okay if your sister and her friend come along to the party isn't it?' and Tad lets out this groan, like, 'do they have to?', only I know he doesn't mind because we had gone out with him and his uni friends before. They were mostly stuck up, but I started hanging around them more and more after that because of Konrad. He was stuck up a little too except he was so charming at first that you didn't mind. I mean, I used to like the way he was a little bit arrogant. It made him look confident.

I fell in love with him that night. I know most people say that there isn't such a thing as love at first sight but I think there is. I have this theory that we're like ducks and geese and things: we wait for someone to come along that has all the right points – and then our mind makes this decision, 'He's the guy!' and that's it. We're stuck with the decision because it's a chemical thing. That's why it's called falling in love. Anyway, that's what I think happened to me and Konrad. It wasn't just that he was cute – he was the type of guy that you could actually talk to. He told me about himself a lot, about how he was studying law but didn't like it. About how his Dad was a lawyer and wanted Konrad to be just like him. He liked me too, I could feel it. It's just that some people are so full of pressures. His parents didn't expect him to go out with someone like me.

I didn't think about that at the time though. I'm the type of person that makes up their mind about what they want then gets it. Mum always says I'm like a bull terrier in that way. I'm also the type of person that waits until things are perfect before going for something. That's why I hadn't had a boyfriend before Konrad. I wanted to find the right guy. I was always getting teased about it by Sandra but I didn't care. Sometimes we would go out and a boy would try to kiss me and I could smell all the alcohol on his breath and his sweat and feel all the prickles on his face. It was gross. I'm still like that now, you know. I haven't had a boyfriend since Konrad. I wouldn't want anyone to know that because they wouldn't understand.

After that first party I had this dream about Konrad, though I don't remember exactly what happened in it. It was something about meeting Konrad at uni and him taking my hand. All I know is that I woke up feeling all soppy and the feeling stayed with me all day. I could hardly wait until I saw him again.

I went out a lot with Konrad after that. I mean, it wasn't as if he asked me out or anything: we went out to nightclubs, parties, shows, just about everywhere with the group. He would sit next to me and we would dance a lot. He was quite a good dancer and he always picked me. Even if we were dancing in a group he would look at me. I think one of the reasons I fell in love with him was because he made me feel special. Everyone knew we were 'an item' and Sandra would say things like, 'Konrad's coming tonight,' or 'I don't know if Konrad likes that colour.'

I used to day-dream a lot about him. I used to imagine all sorts of stupid things. I'm embarrassed to tell you about them. Mostly it would be things like he would come and pick me up at work in a fancy car and all the people would ask who he was, and I would say, 'He's my boyfriend, didn't I tell you?' and stuff like that. Sometimes the dreams would just go on and on. Like, in some he would propose to me on a yacht and I would quit work and we would get married live in a big house and have kids. Sometimes I would go back to the beginning and think of ways we would get together. In some I was a kind of businesswoman with degrees and everything and we would meet in some professional environment and he would be surprised. Then he would ask me out to lunch and I would drag it on a bit and make him feel sorry that he didn't ask me out when he had the chance. He would come and apologise and tell me how he loved me and I would forgive him. Then it would start all over again with the yacht, the house and kids. Embarrassing.

Then one night we went to The Subway and Konrad was dancing with me on one of the crowded dance floors. I could feel this tension in the air. Suddenly Konrad grabs my hand in his and takes me down to a little room where there's this guy playing a guitar in the corner. The lights are soft and low and I can tell he wants to say something. I am thinking, 'This is it. He's going to ask me out.' Only he didn't and I realised that he was shy, which made me love him all the more. We sat there and spoke about the guitar man in the corner. Konrad said he didn't like him but I knew he was just nervous and needed something to say. He took my hand again and we went back upstairs. I was really happy because he didn't need to say any more.

I understood him perfectly. We both wanted to be alone. When we were leaving the nightclub Konrad and I told the others that we were going to go home because we had enough. I still remember Sandra smiling at me with this teasing look, and raising her eyebrows. I didn't care though. Sandra was just like that.

After that we went back to his place. Konrad used to live with his parents in Dalkeith, except they were away in Europe and he had the house all to himself. I'm glad I didn't meet Konrad's Dad. He sounded like he was really up himself. His Mum sounded like a real ice queen. I could just imagine her all made up, sitting in some Claremont café with the other yuppie ladies, putting on all these airs and graces before driving off in her BMW.

I always feel ashamed when I go into a place like that. It wasn't like Sandra's house which looked old and had lots of odds and ends on the walls and junk lying about. Konrad's place was so neat you were afraid to walk on the carpet. Everything was so white that it didn't look lived in. It was like something out of a glossy magazine. I suppose I should have realised then and there that Konrad and I weren't meant to be together. We were just too different. But all I was thinking about was how this was the best night of my life. I had these butterflies in my stomach and a warm feeling I can still remember whenever I think about it. He was so sweet, the way he made out he could read palms, then said: 'Your hands are so cold, let me warm them up for you.'

The silly fool didn't even know it was my first time. After that I thought it was all official. I called Sandra the next day and we talked about it for hours. I was so excited. I thought he would call me that day but he never did. I waited until Monday and called him. His parents were back and his Mum answered – she said he had gone to uni. She sounded like a real bitch so I didn't even leave a message. I must've called him a dozen times in the next week but he was never there. I just didn't know what to think. At first I thought it was just that he was busy or something. Then I started to worry that he didn't want to speak to me. I tried calling Sandra too to see if she would ask Tad about it and eventually Tad came back and said that Konrad was doing his exams. I knew that wasn't the only thing. I felt sick for a while, I really did. I kept hoping he would call me. When I told Mum about it she was really cruel. All she said was 'I told you so.' She would have flipped if she knew I slept with him.

A couple of weeks later I went to see a movie with some people from work and I saw him coming out with this slim dark-haired girl, all made up and sophisticated. She looked just like Konrad's Mum from the pictures at his house, except younger. He was laughing and carrying on but she was just smiling as if she was afraid to crack her make-up or something. I wanted so much to stop them seeing me, but it wasn't possible. They were coming straight towards us and the bitch practically bumped into me. Suddenly Konrad looked at me as if he's seen a ghost or something and stepped back a little.

'Marta... how are you?' I could see he was really uncomfortable. I just looked at him really cool and said, 'Fine, how are you?' and he said some dumb things for a while. All the time the bitch was looking bored. She didn't even look at me.

'I'd like you to meet Leila,' he said, and the bitch gave me this really fake smile that only lasted two seconds and looked away again. We made some small talk for a few minutes and then Leila tugged him on the sleeve and said, 'We'll be late Konrad.'

'Oh of course! I completely forgot. Look Marta, we've

got to go, so keep well and say hi to the old gang if you see them, okay?' They walked off and I could see Leila was whispering something into Konrad's ear, then the bitch started giggling. Konrad laughed too. I know it was about me.

Sometimes I think he never liked me, that he was just using me for sex. I get really upset when I think of that. But then I remember how special that evening was and I know it was his parents and the pressures and that. We weren't meant to be together, Konrad and me: I wasn't one of them. I loved him and I also hated him. I loved him because of that chemical thing. I hated him because he wasn't mature enough to stand up to his parents and his friends – to realise that we should be together. I hated him because he didn't care about my feelings.

It was so weird. There I was standing in the shower at Marta's house, savouring the rush of the water and wondering what the hell I was doing and what Leila would think if she found out. I began rehearsing a speech, protesting the innocence of it all, but deep down I knew she wouldn't buy it. Like it or not, the old sexual tension between Marta and me was still there. Marta knew it too. When I suggested that Leia would get suspicious, she cut through all the crap.

'You're supposed to be at a tutorial,' she said, probing me with the same matter-of-fact look she had that night outside The Subway five years before. I decided not to be unfaithful to Leila, despite the clear messages Marta was giving me. I thought I was in control of the situation. I must confess though that my resolve began to thaw in the steamy warmth of the bathroom.

I remember drying myself and poking my head around the corner of the door into the tired looking hallway, all wallpapered in some kind of floral print from the fifties. My clothes were gone – on the door handle she had left me an old overcoat of the same vintage: the kind you see suspicious men wearing around public parks. It was warm though: filled with down and softly lined. I felt a bit of an idiot putting it on, particularly as it hung above my knees, but when Marta came out from the kitchen she looked at me as if I was the most natural sight in the world. She had changed into one of those bath robes and had towel-dried her hair. She definitely had an appeal: cute but not pretty. She still had that plumpness in her cheeks, the roundness in her figure and the smoothness in features. It was the kind of appeal that my father once warned me about, the kind that derives mostly from youth. 'Not the kind of girl one marries,' he used to say. I've had my fair share of disagreements with the old man over the years, though I can appreciate now that he has a certain wisdom in him.

'Come into the lounge,' she said, tossing back her hair and walking through a doorway and I did as I was told.

You can always tell what women are really like when you see them in their own homes, where they are mistresses of their own domains. Elsewhere they put on a bit of a show. In public Marta was always smiling sweetly and acting helpless. Yet here in her own home it was clear that she had things well and truly under control. The dimmed lights, the soft music and the woman on the sofa, all disheveled and smelling of fresh soap, certainly had an effect on me. Looking back to the earlier days I realise that even then she was hunting for a man, any man. Her helpless routine was a bit of a trap. Marta is the type of girl that is used to getting exactly what she wants and I realise that she must have been quite upset when she didn't get me all those years before. On that night however the plan was working, at least to some extent.

'I made you some soup,' she said pointing to the steaming mug on the coffee table. I noticed that she left space for me to sit next to her.

'You have a nice place,' I said. It was one of those old crappy places with poky little rooms that always look dark and clammy even in bright summer days – with neighbours so close you can always smell their cooking.

'It's my Mum's,' said Marta. I took a sip of the soup and burnt my tongue.

'I'm sorry, I forgot to warn you. It's a bit hot.'

'That's okay.' We sat there on the sofa in awkward silence for a while longer – she simply stared ahead, while I rolled my tongue around hoping the feeling would come back.

'Did you want something else to drink? Mum's got some red wine.' Marta probably noticed I hadn't touched the cup-a-soup again.

After she got me some red wine I tried to kindle the conversation but it was hopeless. It ended up being the usual interrogation. I said: 'Feels just like old times Marta. Remember those days? We were quite a pair on the old dance-floor weren't we?'

'Yes. I suppose we were.'

'Do you ever see any of the old gang? You were best friends with Tad's sister weren't you?'

'Sandra and I sort of drifted apart. She moved up to the northern suburbs somewhere.'

'Yes I know. I caught up with Tad the other day. He's married to Isabella, did you know?'

'Really?'

I remember leaning back on the sofa next to Marta, feeling the warmth, the wine and the redness in my cheeks. She was sipping delicately on her soup, her knees up to her chest. I could sense tension in the air: an expectancy from her and an awkwardness from me. At that moment I understood that in our own ways we were both trying to recapture the past, me with my university foray and Marta with her man trap. The past however was gone and neither of us could retrieve it. Realising all this brought a curious mix of emotions to well within me. I could remember the old times, the excitement of experimenting with adulthood – and for that I had a surge of affection. Poor Marta didn't know when to give up. It was all so desperate. For that I had sympathy. I had come to terms with the past. Marta had not.

I couldn't help reaching up and touching her cheek. It was spontaneous. She stiffened immediately and moved back, in much the same way as she did at my parents' place before we slept together. I moved away sensing that it was the right thing to do.

My problem is that I sometimes talk too much. At some early parties I practically told Marta my life story. That night was no exception. If only I had shut up and gone home, I'm sure nothing would have happened. Instead I poured myself some more wine and tried to talk honestly.

'I was thinking of that night we spent together.'

'I don't want to talk about that.' She was looking away.

'Marta, we both know what's going on here. We're both adults. I just wanted to say that things have changed too much. Know what I mean?' Silence. I finished the wine and got up. 'I've got to go. It's getting really late. I don't even know whether Leila will still believe that business about the tutorial!' I was laughing as I spoke. Marta got up too except she didn't laugh – she was staring at me with a fixed expression on her face. I put my hand on her shoulder. Suddenly she slapped my hand away and started screaming.

'Get your hands off me, and get out of this house! Get out of my house! Right now!'

'What the hell... What's got into you? Get a hold of yourself.'

There was more screaming and I became a little annoyed.

'Look, I don't have time for games. Just give me my things and I'll go.'

'Like hell.' She stormed out of the room and I followed her. Unfortunately she was already in the bedroom and had slammed the door by the time I got there. I realised with sinking spirits that all my clothes were drying near her heater in that very room.

'Marta, let me in. Marta, this is crazy. For God's sake let me in!'

'Fuck you, Konrad Gruber.'

I tried the door, but it was locked.

I don't know why I ever invited him in. I suppose I felt sorry for him. Even though he was tall, he looked like a sad little schoolboy, all wet and dirty. Mum says men do that to us: make us feel like mothering them. She says they do it on purpose so they can use us. My Dad was like that, she said. Never did a stitch of housework and always came crying to her if he needed something or if he didn't feel well. Just like a little boy. Well Konrad looked like that. He was going to stand around in his wet gear, dripping all over Mum's new carpet so I said he should go and have a shower. Then he starts with this polite business, making out that he should go home and not inconvenience me. It was all play acting, of course.

While he was in the shower, I went and grabbed Dad's old overcoat he left behind. Dad was quite short but I thought it would be all right to cover Konrad for a while.

I told him to leave his clothes outside the door and that I would hang them up near the heater. I didn't think Konrad would be gross enough to leave me his undies as well, but I took them anyway. I got out of my own wet clothes and put on my nice bathrobe. It covers me from head to toe, so I thought he wouldn't get any funny ideas. I wanted a cup of soup so I made myself one and one for Konrad.

When Konrad came out of the bathroom he looked a real sight, with his silly white legs sticking out and the sleeves creeping up to his elbows. He'd combed his hair neatly though (with Mum's comb!) and he smelt really clean.

'I made you some soup,' I said and he sat down next to me on the lounge, even though I had put his mug near the single-seater. He spread his legs just a little when he sat and I could see his you-know-what. It was really embarrassing, so I just looked away. Then he took a sip of his soup and started coughing and making a scene, wagging his tongue as he jumped up and down.

'Jesus Christ, I've well and truly incinerated my tongue. Quick, do you have some water? For Christ's sake!'

'I'm sorry, I should have warned you. Hold on, I'll get you something.'

'Don't bother, it'll be too late. Really, it doesn't matter.'

'Are you sure?' Konrad sat down and laughed a little, shaking his head at the same time. He was like a little boy, he really was.

'Tell you what, something stronger may do the trick.' He was smiling, rolling his tongue around in his mouth.

'Mum's still got some red wine left from Easter.'

'That'll be fine, great actually. I love red wine.'

So I got him the wine and he settled down after that, talking about Sandra and Tad and the old crowd, asking if

I knew what any of them were doing. Except for Sandra, I hadn't seen any of them for longer than him. I only went out with them to see Konrad in the first place.

After a while Konrad finished his glass of wine and he leaned closer to me. I was starting to get uncomfortable. He just sat there staring at me, then slowly put his arm behind me on the back of the couch.

'Remember how it was in the old days, Marta? We were quite a pair on the dance floor weren't we?' He reached over and touched my cheek. I tried to move away. Konrad stopped to pour himself another glass of wine and I hoped that would be it. Only it wasn't and he quickly leaned back towards me.

'I was thinking of that night we spent together – after we came back from The Subway. You were something else, you know that?'

'I don't want to talk about that, thank you very much.' I gave him this really cold stare even though I was actually quite afraid. He was acting like one of those guys I hate.

'Come on Marta, we both know what all this is about, we're grown-ups.' I didn't say anything and he stood up. At first I thought he was getting ready to leave, but he was smiling that dirty joke smile again. He had his hand on his belt buckle 'I have to go soon. I don't know if Leila will believe the business about the tutorial.'

That's when I stood up and said, 'I think you should leave right now.'

'Come on Marta!' He reached out and put his hand onto my neck. He was going to slip it down further when I slapped it away.

'Get your hands off me and get out of my house!' I said it really calmly, but with this sharp voice.

'What the hell… What's with the games?' He took a step forwards. I didn't know what to do, so I pushed past him and ran for my bedroom. Konrad came after me but I was able to get in and lock the door. I always keep the lock in the door. I don't know why. It's one of those old fashioned locks that you can look through. Konrad came a moment later and tried to open the door.

'For fuck's sake Marta, let me in.'

'No, go away!'

'I just want my things. Just give me my things and I'll go.'

'Like hell.'

'Marta!' Konrad started banging the door. 'GIVE ME MY CLOTHES!'

'Stuff you, Konrad Gruber!'

The room was quiet for a long while and Konrad stood outside the door shaking his head slowly as he examined the overcoat.

'Marta, for the love of Christ, just give me my clothes and I'll go. Marta? Are you there?'

'I'm not letting you in. Go, or I'll call the police.'

'WHAT! Look, I can't go like this. Be reasonable.'

'You can keep the coat. Just go.'

'Now don't do anything stupid. Marta...?'

Acquaintance be forgot

I could smell urine and cigarette smoke in the elevator. Konrad was leaning against the glass tapping his foot and shaking his head. I followed the direction of his gaze to the melted emergency button and the graffiti scratched into the stainless steel. Finger smears obscured my reflection but I could see Konrad's downturned mouth and watched his lips move as he spoke.

'I'd like to catch that wanker. What does he say: 'Chaz sux'? I bet they both suck. Bunch of losers with nothing better to do. I'd give them one hell of a hiding. Then I'd make them clean it up. There's a phone number there isn't there? What do you say we give it a ring hey? See how smart these turkeys really are.' I saw his reflection look at me, straight into my eyes, and I quickly turned away. Konrad snorted and when I looked up his eyes had glazed over. He was still staring into the distance when he spoke *sotto voce*.

'Soon as I make it, I'm out of here. This place is for losers.' The elevator slowed with a whine. I felt my stomach rise before the bell toned and the lift shuddered into position. An eternity passed before the door opened.

I followed him down the corridor: the same stench – green carpet rubbed bare in places, with dark splatter stains – holes kicked into the doors and music pounding from the inside – the smell of frying. Konrad paused next to his door fumbling with his keys, unlocked it and punched his way in. The door was still trembling as I walked through. Konrad threw his keys on the vinyl seat but they slid off.

'Wanna drink? We can watch the fireworks from the balcony if you could be bothered. I don't give a rat's arse either way.' Konrad was in the kitchen at the end of the room, looking into the fridge. 'It's all commercial crap anyhow. Just another day in the year isn't it? People make a big deal but when it comes down to it, it's just an excuse to get pissed.' He threw me a beer and twisted the top of his own. I caught the sweet smell of melted fridge ice and mould. Konrad flopped down on a chair and tilted back his bottle while I lowered myself into a chair opposite him, feeling the vinyl stick to my back and the tightness of my wallet in my jeans front pocket. Konrad was silent for a while, staring into the blank wall. I took a swig of the acid froth. Heavy metal music started thumping on the ceiling and I heard muffled shouts, indistinct swearing.

'Another pathetic party,' Konrad said, covering his eyes. 'Probably better than the one at Tad's anyway. He's such an arse wipe. I'm glad I don't have to go, I'll tell you that. Bloody grateful. They're such a bunch of losers, those people at work. You're new Edin, so I have to warn you.' Something smashed above, more swearing.

'I used to hang out with Tad when he first started at work. He was a young fellow then. I thought he might learn something. He turned into such a wanker. Like the rest of them. Last year they invited me, but I just laughed. Like, as if I would waste my time with them.' I nodded, struggling to remove my wallet.

Konrad got up abruptly, walked into the kitchen and opened a cupboard door. After rummaging for a while amongst the plastic bags he return with a small open bottle, inclined as if to pour. I held out my hand and he tapped on the cola stained glass. A shiny red pill fell into my palm. Konrad shook out one for himself and then, motioning for me to follow, threw it back with his beer.

'Go on. It won't kill you.' He fell back into his chair, gesturing again. I stared at the pill. When I looked up Konrad was still waiting. I put it in my mouth, tasted the M & M coating, then swallowed. He smiled, leaned back and closed his eyes.

'I can't stand druggies. They're all so weak.' With his eyes still closed he gestured in the general direction of the pill bottle on the coffee table. 'I don't need that shit. Sometimes I take one for a bit of a laugh. But I don't need to keep taking them. Druggies are people who don't know when to stop.' I heard the distant pop of the fireworks, random cheers. A woman shrieked drunkenly from above.

'The people at work are jealous. They know I have what it takes and that they don't. You have to laugh.' Konrad raised his beer to his lips. 'I used to go out with Leila, did you know? Gave her a good time. But I was just having fun. She got serious, wanted commitment. I'm a free agent. No one's going to tie me down.' His voice gave way to silence. I felt my world beginning to close in, as if I were being smothered in cotton wool.

'Anyway, she had to be kidding. If I were to commit to someone it wouldn't be her. I would have thought that was obvious. She should have been grateful that I even went out with her.' My beer slipped out of my hand but I realized only after it was pumping its contents onto the floor. Konrad became obscured by the flicker of my eyelashes that smeared the yellow light, then stretched it into wavering beams. When my eyes finally closed under their own weight I saw his after-image slumped in the chair.

'Everyone wants to be important. You ever notice that? Except that people like Tad are never going to be important and that pisses them off. They are always looking for ways of big-noting themselves through work or at bullshit parties where they dance around saying 'look at me, look at me'. I'm not like that. I guess that's why I haven't gone in for fame and that kind of thing. I don't need to keep convincing myself that I'm important.'

There was an increasing brightness behind my closed eyelids, a continuous camera flash, and I had to pry them open to relieve the glare. Konrad was still watching me and holding his beer in his lap. He took a swig in short staccato steps, as if he was under a strobe light. The whiteness flooded back.

'I don't go in for self-deception,' he said from behind the screen. 'You know what I mean? I see these people trying to kid themselves about one thing or another.'

I was falling into billowing silken sheets, falling, falling…

'Take Leila for instance. The other day she started talking about work like it was a big, happy family, saying things like 'We need to do this!' and 'I don't know how they are going to compete with us!' The company doesn't give a shit about her! Next downsizing and she's out on her arse.'

I could hear him as if he were talking through a crackling telegraph wire.

'And I hate the way she suddenly likes footy. Before I dumped her she used to hate footy. Now she's convinced herself she likes it because she's with Tad. What a load of crap!'

I saw the telegraph line stretching into the distance.

'It all comes down to selfishness, the greatest fucking evil of all, in my humble opinion. Well if that's the way it's going to be, I'm also looking out for number one.'

I opened my eyes to the grey pre-dawn light and sat up, feeling the pounding in my head, the stiffness in my neck. Konrad was sleeping, his head tilted back on the chair, mouth gaping wide and hands by his sides, so I unstuck myself from the vinyl as quietly as I could. He did not stir even when my uncertain feet stumbled and kicked the empty beer bottle which resounded musically against the metal chair leg. I was almost at the door when I remembered my wallet on the coffee table.

As I stooped to retrieve it, I noticed Konrad's ashen face in the ray of sunlight that had crept in over the balcony. I saw a pink froth caught like the head of a beer between his nostrils and upper lip. The bottle of pills lay next to my wallet, overturned and empty. When I touched Konrad's skin it felt cold. I jerked my hand away in disgust and scrambled for the safety of the corridor.

I worried someone would see me hurrying from the entrance to the building but the street was quiet and empty. Even so I kept running until I had rounded the corner of the block. There, I paused to recover my breath and savour the fresh easterly before setting off into the littered shadows. I wondered if Tad's party was still going.

The aliens

I never really understood why, but Tad was always moving house – often after a mere few months. Whenever I asked about it, he explained himself in cryptic, hypothetical terms, and I was left even more perplexed. The last time we'd spoken, Tad sensed my scepticism and said: 'Look, I just can't tell you now, okay – it's for your own good,' and so I dropped it – and Tad – to pursue my own life and problems. In any event, he and I had gone our separate ways since university so it was quite easy to let our friendship atrophy.

I had not seen Tad in over a year, when I got a surprise call from his parents who were worried about him.

'He's so irrational nowadays,' they said. 'You were the only one he ever really listened to – he won't even talk with us at all anymore. Could you visit him – see if he's all right?' I said I would.

When I rang Tad I immediately regretted my promise to his parents.

'Tad! It's me, Edin.' I spoke as enthusiastically as I could manage. Tad responded vaguely, as if he were in the middle of something and I had called at a bad time. I explained that I was thinking of popping around to see him and wondered if he would be in.

'Oh… sure… if you like,' he said.

And so there I was on a bright Sunday morning,

apprehensively staring through the gate, wondering if I had made a mistake.

Walking down the musty corridor with its faded blue carpet, dull historical prints and artificial plants I thought that Tad's apartment felt less like a home than a cheap motel: furbished in bad taste because the view of the river was adequate compensation and because nobody cared. As I approached Tad's door I could hear the muffled whine of a vacuum cleaner, punctuated by occasional indistinct voices and the odd thump. I knocked. The sigh of the vacuum's motor was still fading as Tad opened the door.

What shocked me at that moment was not Tad's haggard and unshaven appearance – his deeply sunken eyes regarded me impatiently as if I were an unwelcome door to door salesman – but the scene behind him in the apartment which his body only partly obscured. It was empty save for some boxes stacked in the middle. Tad stood for a moment in the doorway before he moved aside and motioned with his hand.

'Come in,' he said, with a sigh and a voice that echoed in the vacancy. He quickly shifted the vacuum cleaner out of the way and I searched for something to say as I examined the barren room.

'I'm sorry there isn't any where to sit – the furniture's already gone,' he said, combing his hand through his greasy hair with a hand that trembled ever so slightly. Tad was wearing a shirt I had bought for his birthday in our first year at university – only it was now hopelessly out of fashion and too small for him. Outside, through the expansive windows, a demure dark-haired woman in her mid-thirties was strolling along Tad's balcony, a young boy, only partly visible above the window frame, quietly in tow. Behind them I could see the deep blue of the river and the olive green that faded to grey in the hills at the horizon.

'Can I get you some water? I think I still have some glasses.'

'No, I'm fine thanks Tad,' I answered and another awkward silence followed. At length all I could say was: 'You're moving again,' and he nodded.

'Yes, I've found a place in Victoria Park. It's only a bedsitter but it's all I need.' He had his hands in his back pockets as he nervously glanced out at the woman on the balcony. She in turn regarded him – and me – momentarily with a faint, distant smile before turning to survey the view. Her child, a boy of no more than four or five, took her hand and looked away at the same time, their jet black hair blowing gently in the light breeze.

I was unsure of what to do. Logic told me to be diplomatic and gradually broach the subject of his moving but on the other hand I could not think of anything circumspect to say. In the end I simply blurted out: 'I don't understand Tad: your parents told me you had just moved in here. Why the hell are you moving again?' At that moment the pretense of cordiality ended and in a surreal sort of way I found myself having an argument with Tad as if we had never stopped seeing each other. There were no more pleasantries, no small talk – just a continuation of the same dialogue of more than a year before.

'Look, I told you ages ago – I don't have a choice. They're making me.' Tad spoke in a harsh whisper and kept looking towards the woman and child on the balcony, who were still facing away from us towards the river. At the time I was oblivious to his body language – perhaps because what he seemed to be saying was absurd.

'Who's making you Tad? I can't understand who would

want you to move.'

'They are,' said Tad tilting his head in the direction of the woman and child, 'the aliens.'

There comes a point in some arguments where it is useless saying anything further – and yet I always do. This occasion was no exception. It wasn't as if I thought I had a chance of convincing him – it was clear to me that he was quite delusional – and logic, if not experience, told me I didn't stand a chance. However there is something in the human psyche – something I certainly possessed – that makes us want to confront the outrageous, expose it, punish it and thereby triumph over it. I knew it would be a fruitless endeavour, but I felt powerless to stop myself arguing with him.

'Don't be absurd Tad – this whole thing is ridiculous. Can't you see what you're doing to yourself – to your family? Do you know that your parents called me? They're worried about you – they can't sleep at night. And look at you: you spend all of your hard earned money on removalists, bonds and broken lease agreements. Wake up for God's sake!' I raised my voice slightly as I spoke but then turned in embarrassment to see if the woman had heard. Fortunately she continued to gaze out across the estuary, oblivious to our conversation. Tad nodded, twitching and fidgeting.

'Listen to me,' he said lowering his voice even more, 'they are aliens – I have to do this. Can't you see? Look for yourself!' He finished his sentence with a whisper that spat at me and his hand motioned violently towards the window. 'Look!' Outside the window the woman and child were strolling up the length of the balcony, quietly enjoying the view.

'They look like a perfectly ordinary mother and son to me.'

'For crying out loud – can't you see proof when it's staring you in the face?'

'What proof? Get a hold of yourself!'

While Tad stared at me in exasperation, I was suddenly conscious that I had been raising my voice again.

'You must be crazy,' he said after a pause.

'One of us is but it sure as hell isn't me.' I regretted my tone even as I spoke but the old instinct to conquer and suppress would not be denied. I decided to try a different tack.

'You know,' I said gently, 'there are people who can help you with this sort of thing. You don't need to live like this.'

Tad twisted his face into a smile as he shook his head. 'Believe me Edin, I wish I could simply accept I was mad – but it's pretty hard when the obvious is in front of me. Am I really the only person who sees these things?'

A moment of silence followed as the conclusion that we were at an impasse swept me. Not knowing what else to do I decided to humour him a little, so I asked: 'Why do you think they are aliens Tad?'

'They say they are. What else could they be?'

'Well they don't look like aliens.' I ventured.

'It's not how they look – it's what they can do. They can walk on air.' Tad whispered the last sentence as if it was a fact we were both aware of, and with all the passion of an evangelist. I remember thinking how comically absurd the conversation was – how I felt as if I was in some sort of dream, hearing Tad say the things he was saying. I almost thought he would suddenly snap out of it and declare the whole thing a bad joke, but the cold, hard fact of the situation simply excluded this possibility. I was about to suggest that the 'abilities' of the woman and child did not necessarily lead to the conclusion that they were aliens, when a knock on the door saved me from this foolish and condescending idea.

When Tad answered the door I saw an older man with a peppercorn moustache, standing somewhat reluctantly in the hallway – a tall, younger man hovered behind. They were both dressed 'informally' in jeans and long sleeve shirts – a uniform casualness that announced officialdom.

'Can I help you?'

'Are you Tadeusz Jesnoewski?'

'Yes, what's all this about?'

'I'm Dr Max Ackerman and this is Nurse Chaz Amsel. We're from the Psychiatric Emergency Team. I need to speak with you for a moment.'

Tad's brow twisted in consternation and he momentarily turned to me whereupon I shrugged in genuine ignorance.

'Look, what's this all about?'

The doctor appeared apologetic as he explained.

'You see Tadeusz – may I call you Tadeusz? – your mother rang us last night with some concerns about you. She says you are moving again.'

Tad stared at him in a silence before countering:

'So what? It's none of her business – and none of yours.'

'Well Tadeusz, your mother is concerned about your finances – she says you are very badly in debt.'

'That's still none of her business,' Tad said. He was holding the door so firmly I could see his knuckles go white. Both the doctor and nurse were still standing in the corridor and, seeing that Tad was not making any move to let them inside, Dr Ackerman dutifully but uneasily continued with what was obviously an examination. The nurse looked on blankly.

'It's something you told her last night. Apparently you

said some 'aliens' are forcing you to move. Do you really believe that Tadeusz?' Tad glanced furtively over his shoulder and then looked back at Dr Ackerman, lowering his voice as he spoke.

'Look Doctor, you've got to help me get away from them – I can't take it anymore.'

'So you do believe 'aliens' are making you do things?'

'I'm not crazy Doctor – I know what I see! Tell them Edin.' Tad looked at me imploringly and I shifted uneasily.

'I… I'm sorry Tad,' was all I could say.

At that moment I became aware that the woman and child had come in off the balcony and were standing in the far corner of the empty room, watching silently. I tried to catch the woman's eye but she seemed not to notice me at all, observing Tad and the doctor with a curious, detached interest – another spectator to Tad's drama. I wondered momentarily how Tad had met them whether they were aware of his fixation. Tad glanced back.

'Is that them?' Doctor Ackerman indicated with his eyes. Tad's nod was almost imperceptible.

'You must help me,' he whispered.

The doctor pulled out a notebook and wrote something down.

'We can help you Taduesz – but I think you'll have to come with us to the hospital where we can talk about this some more.'

Tad's eyes widened – then he looked down and shook his head.

'What if I don't come with you?'

'Tadeusz, I really think you should. Otherwise I will have to fill out the necessary forms to compel you.' He paused briefly before continuing. 'It means we come back with the police.'

Tad's face twisted into a sneer and he looked back at the woman. Then he slowly picked up his jacket which had been draped over one of the boxes, turned and bowed to the woman and opened his arms to the doctor.

I could not bear to go with them to the waiting vehicle, so I stayed behind while they departed. The mother and son followed quietly. Like Tad, neither acknowledged me as they left. I waited till the footsteps had faded down the corridor and listened for the elevator bell before I let myself breathe again. Then I lowered myself onto one of the sturdy boxes, surveying the largely empty room – mute testimony to Tad's misdirected and futile endeavours. I remember idly wondering if this would be his last move – at least for the foreseeable future. Then, as I rose to leave, I impulsively walked to the window to get a final view of the panorama, framed by the wide panes in the far wall.

Soon after I reached the glass I came to the realization something was horribly wrong. For as I leaned over I could see the majestic river-estuary in all its brilliant blue, hemmed by the well-tended parks and gardens on its banks. Tiny motor vehicles passed each other along the Narrows Bridge like ants in an endless succession, while the modern buildings on the Terrace towered into a sky that was as clear and radiant as it had ever been. Everything was perfect. But there was no balcony.

The mallard

All our lives are ultimately reduced to someone else's memory. This is the thought that occurs to her as she stares out of her kitchen window, past the hazy, beaded glass and into the wetlands, now overgrown with tufts of winter grass. Tad is buried by the brass picture frame lying face down on the cabinet. She has done this to forget, but forgetting is impossible, for the mind is a persistent child who will not be ignored. Nor can she resist the urge to lift the picture (as she does now) to caress his smiling cheek through the glass.

She remembers the day of the picture. They had come back from the usual madness of his parents' house, where he and his younger brothers laughed and wrestled with each other while his mother and sister talked quietly in the tiny kitchen. That left her with the old man who spoke meditatively, his eyes always focused dimly on a homeland far removed in geography and time. She'd snapped Tad as he stepped out of their first car, their brand-new, second-hand bomb that exploded only months later. She'd captured the full force of his startle and had it framed.

She returns the picture to its position on the cabinet but doesn't bother to turn it over. Instead she picks up the vase Max had given her that morning and examines it carefully. Her uncle runs a little bric-a-brac store on the other side of the lake. It is an old part of town with narrow streets, cracked pavements and sedate trees, pruned and gnarled into strange shapes because of the overhead lines. Uncle Max's shop-front fits in perfectly with its art deco facade, boxed awning and peeling paint. As you look through the bay windows you are confronted with someone else's myriad jumbled, faded memories: from the tartan lampshade to the yellowed sewing machine – from the dusty black typewriter to the dog-eared Nat King Cole record sleeves and leather covered books high up on the shelf.

'You need to get out more,' Max always tells her, so she goes to visit him on Saturday mornings rather than do the chores and watches as he laughs with the customers.

When she opened the jingling door that morning he said 'I have something for you,' and placed the vase in her hands so she could feel the weight and texture of the stained glass ridges. 'It's magic, you know.'

'I could do with some magic,' she said laughing, but Max looked on seriously and she remembered just how superstitious he was.

'That vase can bring you happiness. That's something you deserve.'

'I am happy Uncle Max.'

'What nonsense,' he snorted before turning to a customer, leaving her fingering the cool, dark glass and the undulating rim of the lip and staring at the stained picture of a green-headed duck. Max returned to her a moment later and said 'You need to make a wish,' but she smiled wryly and shook her head. Then, as now, her knuckles went white.

She grips the vase as she looks back out of the window to the marsh. A solitary figure moves silhouetted against the reeds and, in an agonizing moment, she recognizes his shock of dark hair. It happens all the time: in supermarkets and shopping malls, while waiting in a queue for movie tickets or walking to the bus stop. Sometimes it's the smell of his cologne, sometimes the sound of his laugh. In every case he disappears just as soon as she catches up to him, the fading end of a rainbow.

'It's a form of self-torture,' said Stan when he and Marcin came to visit. Marcin added, 'We don't mind if you go out with someone. Really, we don't. And Tadeusz would have wanted it. The grieving time is over, you know.' She did know. She learned all the rules of Tad's culture only to remain an outsider. Now that her nexus to his family had been broken they have drifted even further apart. Tad's brothers haven't visited again and she only sees his sister, Sandra, because they work together. What would they, anyone, think of her now as she carefully replaces the vase and goes to the hall cupboard to get her rain jacket?

Outside she feels the sting of rain in her eyes and the wet lick of the long grass against her jeans as she approaches him. He is walking away, moving behind a thicket of reeds, down to the water. As she reaches the crest of the bank she sees he has gone, absorbed into the shadows. She scans in both directions as far as the dim light will allow but there is nothing. For a while she feels a blow, like a punch to the solar plexus, like remembering your keys are in the ignition just as you lock the door, like opening a letter of rejection. Finally, the sense of urgency drains to the familiar, bone-dry emptiness, and the only goose bumps left are those from the cold.

She turns, alerted by the squelch of shoes, to see a man approaching. He is not Tad: he is taller, with olive skin, dark hair, a bronze stubble and eyes that squint against the drizzle. She wants to avoid him but it's too late. He has seen her, the only other person on the open space. Besides that, he greets her with a 'Hello!' and a smile.

'Hi…'

'Out for a walk?' He is still smiling, ignoring the elements.

'Yes.'

'Lovely weather for it.' He turns to the sky, laughing, his mouth open as if to catch the rain.

'Well, I'd better…' She is backing away when he speaks.

'See that?' He points to the swamp where the rain spits ringlets around the lazy swans while the ducks, geese and coots huddle on the banks. 'That one there with the green head.'

She follows the outstretched finger and says 'Oh yes.' Then the duck raises its head momentarily above its mottled grey brethren and she sees the white neck band.

'That's a mallard drake. *Anas platyrhynchos*. It shouldn't be here. It's an introduced species, from the Northern hemisphere.'

'How?'

'Who knows? The problem is they breed with the local Black ducks.' He turns back to her. 'Just another way the exotics displace our native fauna.' He is looking at her now, as if in recognition. 'Do you live nearby?'

'Yes.' She points vaguely to the ridge of houses encircling the marsh.

'I must have seen you here before.'

'Probably. Anyway…' The rain abruptly builds to a crescendo, beating down hard on their heads and shoulders, drops the size of golf balls, and they both look up foolishly.

'Enjoy your walk.' He is laughing again, his voice

almost drowned by the white noise.

So the duck has a name. Isabella holds the vase in her hands while she drips pools on the polished wooden floor. Outside the rain blankets the marsh in an opaque haze.

'Who's the lucky guy?'

'Eh?' Isabella startles out of her dream and turns to her colleague.

'That look on your face and the way you had your chin cupped in your hand. You've found a guy.'

'Don't be ridiculous Sandy.'

'Come on, tell me.'

'There is no guy.'

'Hm. You know what? I believe you. That's the sad part.'

'Oh please. I've got to get back to work.'

'Your life has to start again sometime. You know what the Chinese say?'

Isabella sighs. 'Okay, tell me. What do the Chinese say?'

'A storm never lasts all day. Your storm's gone on way too long.'

'You read too many new age books.'

'I bought that one from your uncle's shop.'

'Look, I've really got a lot on right now.'

'Whatever.' Sandra starts walking out. 'Oh, and by the way, you might want to scroll down to page two. You've been on page one all day.'

Isabella turns to the computer monitor, cursing the fact that she sits with her back to the door. Bad feng shui, says Sandra and in this case she is probably right. 'Hey wait!'

'Yes, Snookums.' Sandra's face appears from behind the door frame.

'Come in and close the door.'

'Ah, ha.' She rubs her hands. 'I knew something was

up.'

'Nothing's up.'

'Sure. Just spill the beans,' says Sandra as she pulls up the chair on the other side of Isabella's desk.

'It's no big deal really.'

'I'm waiting.'

'Well,' Isabella feels her cheeks warming up, 'I feel stupid. Anyway, Uncle Max gave me this vase on Saturday.'

'Mmm. And this means...' Sandra waves her hand in a circle.

'Nothing, really. Max had some idea that it could grant wishes.'

'Like a genie?'

'Yeah, whatever.'

'And let me guess, you were wishing for...' Sandra pauses for a moment, then gives Isabella a wry look. 'You never learn, do you.'

'It's just that I think I saw him.'

'He can't come back! He's gone.' Sandra lowers her voice and reaches out to touch her shoulder. 'You have to face that and move on.'

'I know, I know.' Isabella turns back to the computer screen, now blurred and shimmering. 'You know, yesterday I tried to remember his face and I couldn't. I had to look at a picture...' The screen saver comes on. Sandra's hand is still on her shoulder but Isabella is alone.

Her hands hold up the vase to the reading lamp so that the light scatters and skews, twisting the room into an hallucinogenic blur. She turns to the window and watches the swamp through the vase, catching the last rays of the sun. A dark smudge makes her lower it.

She doesn't remember how she got there, but she is

walking through the damp grass, feeling the chill creeping in with the shadows. The smell of dank water and mud mixes with that of log fires and evening meals from the cosy houses, where the lights glow softly and televisions flicker. He is seated on the bank with his back turned to her, a sprig of grass twitching like a whisker from one side of his mouth.

'Hello…'

He turns around in a leisurely way, a small smile on his lips, as if he were expecting her. 'Hi again.' He is wearing a denim jacket, upturned against the cold and the light catches one side of his face. Then he turns back to look at the swollen swamp, where reeds like needles puncture its glassy surface and paperbark trees huddle and tread water in the shallows. He shakes his head. 'Every winter, after the rains, the ducks leave. They go to the wheat belt, where the lakes have filled up for a while.'

'Do they come back?'

'Not always. Look, there's that mallard.'

'How do you know it's the same one?'

'Oh, it's him alright.' He flicks a pebble into the water and ducks rush to the ripples. His dark eyes focus directly on hers. 'You can just tell – can't you?' Isabella nods and crouches down on the bank, feels the wet blades of grass with her fingertips.

'How do they know to come back? The ducks, I mean.'

'They're not migratory. Not in the true sense of the word. But they find their way, like many species of bird. It's one of those mysteries of nature that shouldn't be solved. What would life be like if we knew everything, if there was no… magic?' He takes a deep breath of the cold air. 'You know, this reminds me of when I was little. We'd play soccer outside until it got too dark to see the ball and one of us was always late for dinner.' He gets up and stretches and she follows. 'I'll see you 'round, I suppose.'

'Yes, see you…'

Isabella watches him walk along the bank and blend into the shadows. Just like Tad had moments before.

The door makes a loud jingle as she opens it. Uncle Max is at the back of the store on a step ladder, putting books onto a shelf. He stares down at her over the top of his reading glasses and his moustache twists up at the corners. 'Ah, my favourite niece.'

'Hi there Max.'

'Any luck yet?'

'Sorry?'

'The vase. Any luck with vase?' He starts climbing down. 'I'm expecting big things from it you know.'

'Do you mean, has it brought me happiness? No. Not yet anyway.'

'Maybe you're not asking for the right things.'

'You've been speaking to Sandra, haven't you?'

'Well, she did come in this morning.'

'I should have known.'

'Steady on. She's your friend and she's worried about you.'

'I know, I know. It's just that…' Max sits in the bay window, pats the cushion and she joins him.

'You were saying?'

'Max, do you think I'm going crazy?'

'Maybe.'

'That's not what I wanted to hear.'

'What is crazy? I'm not sure any more. All I know is that everyone experiences a unique reality.'

'And you think my reality is skewed,' she says, looking away. Max shakes his head and strokes her hair.

'No, no, I just think it's different. At least for now. It'll change when the time is right.'

'Look, maybe I am seeing things. Maybe Tad can't come back. Maybe on one level it's impossible. All I know is that on some other level, it's as if he never left.' Max says nothing but leans forward, tweaking his moustache. 'I keep having these dreams. Tad is sitting around talking to me. It's like, the most ordinary thing in the world. Then suddenly I realize something's wrong, that he's not meant to be here. Whenever I ask him how it's possible, he just laughs, as if I already know the answer. Or maybe there is no answer.' Isabella looks down at her hands in her lap, notices they are trembling.

'Or maybe the answer is not important,' Max says covering them with his own.

She awakes. Tad is lying next to her, eyes open, smiling, waiting for a kiss. She reaches for his face but it fades, crumbles into pixels. His side of the bed is empty and cold: reality has taken his place.

Isabella can no longer sleep, so she walks into the kitchen to make herself a cup of coffee and look out of the window. This was Tad's morning ritual: he would always get up just before sunrise and stand, often stark naked, looking out into the milky, monochrome half-light. Sometimes she would join him and put her hand on his shoulder but he would not seem to notice. After about five minutes he would make himself breakfast, iron his shirt, shave, make loud, disgusting noises in the bathroom. But he never mentioned what he saw out of the window. Perhaps it was something she could never see. His own reality.

Isabella shivers, expecting to see him there, but he is not. Only his picture, which is still displayed on the cabinet, declares his presence with an explosive smile. The dull, opaque vase stands mute next to him. She walks up to it and stares into the obsidian silence, holds it up to the window, but the vase still refuses to reveal its mysteries. She feels the weight, traces the raised outline of the mallard.

When she looks up Tad is waiting on the marsh, slouching in his familiar way. He is looking back at the house, back at her. Beckoning. Or saying goodbye. Her hands begin to shake and she looks down at the vase.

Then she lets it slip, feeling her fingers sliding up to the rim followed by the sudden loss of weight on her palms. She watches as it falls, almost in slow motion, to the floor, expects the vase to bounce, but instead sees it shatter into a thousand pieces that scatter across the room, under the cabinet and out into the hallway.

Isabella is running, sliding in the wet clay and flattened grass, panting fog. The breaking light cruelly stings her eyes. When she arrives, breathless, the lake is deserted. A lone coot pecks its way through the black mud – even the ducks have gone. She sits down on the slope, the dew bleeding into her jeans, but she doesn't care.

'Hello.' Isabella looks up to see the stranger, huddled, hands in pockets. 'I'm sorry, I didn't mean to startle you. I was just wondering if you were okay.'

'Yes, sure. I'm fine.' She combs the hair from her face and wipes the corners of her eyes. 'I didn't expect you... anyone... to be here.'

'At least our friend is still with us,' he says pointing to the swamp where the mallard has emerged from the reeds. 'Anyway...' He waves and starts to back away. Isabella gets up.

'I thought he'd gone. You know, to the wheat belt.'

'Oh, I think he would have left by now. He'll probably

stay on through the winter. Like you and me, I guess.'

She wipes her muddy hands on her jeans.

'I'm Isabella,' she says, extending her hand. He smiles as he shakes it.

'Edin.'

'You seem to know a lot about birds,' she says with a croaky voice, then clears her throat. 'Are you an ornithologist?'

'No, no. Strictly an amateur. I was just trying to impress you with my general knowledge. Actually I'm a writer. I come out here to collect my thoughts – sometimes I write whole chapters in my mind.' He pauses briefly, looks down. Isabella watches him tracing a line in the clay with his shoe. 'You know that café just over the lake?' He points. 'I could buy you a cup of coffee or something. I prefer tea, personally.' Isabella hesitates as she remembers the broken glass littering her cold, empty house.

'Oh… Um, I have some things… to do.' He quickly motions that it's okay. 'No, really,' she continues. 'Just… not today. I mean, can I take a rain check?' Edin chuckles, studies her frowning face then says gently:

'Sure. Anytime Isabella.' He makes a small, awkward wave and turns.

'Hey Edin… I'll see you?' He looks back and nods, a flash of white teeth, his eyes squinting in the morning rays.

All our lives are ultimately reduced to someone else's memory. This is the thought that occurs to her as she watches Edin retreating into the morning shadows. The day is warming up. Max's shop opens soon, but she might catch him some other time.

Hotel forever

'Have you ever thought that life is just like a holiday? I mean, you spend half your time worrying about not doing anything exciting, the other half doing things you don't really want to. Before you know it, it's over. You've wasted it.'

'Don't get depressing Edin, I can't cope with it now.' Isabella didn't look up from the wheel as she spoke but her dark eyes glared under her furrowed brow. I said nothing for a moment and slouched back in my seat. 'I'm really am sick and tired of you sulking whenever it comes to getting together with my family. If you didn't want to come, why didn't you just say so?

'I'm only home for a few weeks. Why would I spend it all by myself in a little apartment while you're off at some resort having fun with a hundred relatives?'

Isabella exhaled and her eyes went wide. 'I don't believe it! First you say that my family is taking you away from your writing. Now you don't want to be left out of the fun. Which is it? You can't have it both ways.'

'What do you expect me to do? I'm only human. I need company too you know.'

'Poor Edin. I thought you liked being alone. You just about tear my head off if I so much as make a sound while you're writing.'

'Okay. But that doesn't change the fact that it's work,

not fun. I also need time to relax. You know, 'all work and no play …'.'

'Except you're always dull.'

'What was that?'

'Nothing.'

'I work damn hard Issy. The least you could give me is a little respect. I'm not asking for much.'

'What? When do I disrespect you? I never complain about the compromises to our lives – the fact that you're away for months at a time. I don't recall saying a word about the fact that when you're back, you're mostly glued to your computer damn screen. I tolerate ridiculous bans on guests during the day as well as temper tantrums, agonies and all-round pathos every time you experience some kind disappointment. Get real, Mister! What the hell do you think I'm supposed to do for the rest of my life? Give up every social engagement and every hobby that interferes with your 'creative flow'?'

I said nothing.

We climbed over a rise and a pocket of flickering lights came into view on the left. Isabella swung the car into a long, winding driveway where the gravel popped beneath the wheels. Eventually we came to a roughly hewn, limestone building nestled among giant fig trees and pulled into one of the car bays under the yellow lamps. A broad sign across the entrance proclaimed 'Casa Eternidad'.

'There's Konrad and his girlfriend: what's her name?'

'Leila. As if you don't remember! You couldn't take your eyes off her at Easter.'

'Now come on – that's a lie! Uh oh, he's seen us.' I covered my face.

'Oh for Heaven's sake! Konrad is supposed to be *your* friend – remember?'

'Yeah well... we were friends in uni, but he's always been an arrogant prick – I just didn't see it back then. As near as I can tell, he's gotten worse. Much worse. God knows what Leila sees in him.'

'Someone might ask what I see in you. Anyway, enough of that. Try to enjoy yourself.'

I grimaced.

'They're waving. Wave back. Go on.'

'I am. I am.' I performed a royal wave. 'Grist for my writing I suppose,' I said, watching them as they disappeared into the crowd milling at the main entrance.

'That's right. Look on the positive side,' said Isabella as she opened her door and stepped out. I followed her.

At that moment a man with a thick moustache the colour of white pepper stepped out from the crowd, smiling broadly and holding his arms apart.

'Uncle Max!' Isabella said, wrapping her arms around him.

'And how is my favourite niece? I shouldn't say that too loudly, should I? I mean the others are nearby.' He turned to me and extended his hand. 'I see you've brought your writer husband, though he is looking under the weather today.'

I shook his hand. 'How are you Max?'

'Couldn't be better. Come inside.' He let his niece hook his arm and placed his other hand on my shoulder. 'They only finished restoring it two months ago. Charming isn't it? Ah! I see Konrad and Leila – I must go and say hello.'

He patted Isabella's hand as he extricated himself and we followed him through the foyer into a room enclosed by pressed tin walls and heavy jarrah roof beams. A number of people were occupying leather lounge chairs and as we approached one of them, a thin, sickly man with greasy hair, stood up.

'Tad is here,' I said quietly.

'Be nice. If I can, so can you.'

'I'm afraid I've lost all patience with him. The man's a total a nut-job – a waste of space and air.'

'What a horrible thing to say! Especially about someone you grew up with – someone who has been like a brother to you.' Tad was getting nearer and Isabella dropped her voice to a hoarse whisper, saying: 'Remember: it isn't his fault he has a mental illness. If anything, you're at least partly to blame – or are you still trying to argue that the drugs you and Konrad were giving him back in uni didn't contribute to his current condition?' She glared at me before turning to her ex-husband, saying, animatedly: 'Tad, how are you?' He sidled up, tried to kiss her on the mouth but she turned her head so his lips met her cheek. Then he hugged her – a little too long and a little too closely for my liking. I was glad Issy's baby bump forced a least a bit of space between them.

'Yeah – I'm okay. I guess,' he said, letting his arms flop down to his sides. He looked at his shoes and said to me: 'Hi Edin. How's... the writing going?'

'Great.'

'That's good,' he mumbled. Abruptly he looked up at Isabella, clasped his hands together and announced: 'Hey listen, we've had a wonderful idea! We're going down to the beach and lighting up a fire. We'll take some drinks down and Konrad has his guitar, though God save us if he starts to sing. It should be bags of fun.'

'Who's going?' asked Isabella.

'All the so-called younger set, you know: my brothers, Marta, Chaz, and so on. Even Sandra's tagging along. The old fogies are staying here.'

'Count me in with the old fogies,' I said to no one in

particular. I don't know why I did that. I certainly wasn't relishing the thought of trying to chat with Tad's elderly parents, whose contempt for me had become barely-veiled since I'd 'stolen away' their former daughter-in-law.

Tad said: 'It's a fair hike Issy, so we had better get going. They rest have already headed off.'

'Why don't you come, Edin? Please?' Isabella looked at me as if to say: '*Stop being an arsehole.*'

'No, I think I'll stay. Really. You go on ahead. I catch you later.' She pursed her lips and frowned at me before following Tad out through the back patio.

I made my way to where Max was sitting and talking animatedly with a lean, angular-featured man with greying hair. A young girl was hanging off the man's arms, pouting.

'Edin, meet Dan. He's an old friend of mine,' said Max, gesturing to companion. We shook hands while the girl was tugging on Dan's sleeve.

'Daddy...'

'Good to meet you Edin.'

'Daddy pleeease...'

'Okay, okay Maya. Hold your horses,' Dan said to his daughter. Then he turned to us, smiled apologetically and said: You'll have to excuse me for just a moment.'.

'Of course! You'd better see what the emergency is,' replied Max, laughing as Dan was dragged into the corridor.

Once they were gone Max said: 'We were just discussing the mysterious history of this place.'

'Oh?' I lowered myself into a chair.

'Absolutely fascinating. Do you know what 'Eternidad' means?'

'It's Spanish for 'eternity'.'

'That's right. It seems the Benedictines sent three

Spanish monks up here to found the settlement. For a couple of years everything seemed to be going well. They made friends with the local Aboriginals, started some vegetable patches. Then one day a supply coach came up and there was no one here. Even the Aboriginals had gone. It was as if they had vanished into thin air.'

'What happened to them?'

'No one knows. Their final journal entry was just one word: 'Eternidad'. Probably went mad, ran off into the bush and died.'

'That's quite a story.'

'Isn't it! Maybe something you might want to write about!' He laughed. 'I see you're not impressed. Tell me, what do you write about Edin?'

'I'm working on some science fiction stories at the moment.'

'Never had much time for that. Ray guns and what have you. Why do you do it?'

'I happen to think science fiction is a worthwhile genre…'

'No, I mean why write at all? I mean, it's not as if anyone reads any more. I haven't read fiction in years.'

'I write because I have something to say.'

'Suppose no one wants to listen? Kids nowadays either can't read, or prefer to sit in front of a computer or look at their phones. The rest of us are too busy.'

'There will always be people who read.'

'That number is getting smaller and smaller, as are your chances of being published. Anyway have you had a look at what people are reading? Fat political thrillers, historical romances. All formula stuff. Nobody is saying anything. They're just providing a form of escapism. Personally, I'd rather escape at the cinema.'

'That doesn't worry me.'

'It should. Writing looks like hard work. You ought to have some reason for doing it.'

'How about art for art's sake?'

'Nonsense! You mean to tell me that you would write something even if you knew no one was ever going to read it?'

'Yes...'

'Humph. Art is about people. It's about ego. It's about showing off. Art is just as competitive and goal directed as sport or climbing the corporate ladder. Without an audience or rival, art is meaningless.'

'Come off it! Art is a process as much as a goal. I enjoy the act of writing...'

'Then, dear Edin, why aren't you happy?'

'I am.'

'You can kid yourself, but you can't kid me.'

'Look, Max. Writing isn't always a barrel of laughs. But that's life. I don't always enjoy going for a jog, but I'm usually glad I did it at the end.'

'I hate jogging at any time. However let's explore the analogy. If writing is like jogging and you're only happy after you've written something, then surely the thing you like about writing is the result and not the process?'

'Maybe...'

'And what use is the result if you don't have someone to share it with? Like I said, writing is showing off. It's about the need to feel important. The need to be loved.'

'You make it sound like writing is hedonistic.'

'Of course it is. Everything we do is for self-gratification. What's wrong with that anyway? I can see you don't believe me. Well I used to think like you do. Over time I learned differently. You might see me as cynical or negative. But the way I see it, I'm really just you – twenty years later.'

I got up.

'This is all very interesting Max, but I think I'll go find Isabella and the others.'

'Good idea. Go find some people. Get involved in the real world.' Max smiled.

'Yeah, right,' I said, then turned and walked toward the door to the patio. I noticed that the lounge was now empty except for Max who remained meditatively in his seat holding his clasped hands under his nose.

Outside the night had finally closed in. A few patrons still braved the mosquitoes and the gathering chill, sipping pre-dinner drinks. I didn't recognise any of them so I approached a waiter who was wiping one of the bench tops.

'I'm looking for my wife and some of her relatives. A group of people. One had a guitar.'

'Sorry sir.'

'They said they were going down to the beach. Can you tell me how to get there?'

'Sure. See that path? Follow it down through those trees.'

'Thanks.'

As I stumbled through the world of indigo I could just make out the path leading up to the dunes. I slipped and clawed my way to the top expecting to see a distant fire or hear the faint strumming of a guitar but was instead confronted with an empty shoreline stretching into the darkness and the pounding froth of the Guinness-like waves.

When I returned to the patio, I saw that it had been deserted. The lounge was also empty, save for the waiter quietly removing glasses on a silver tray. Dan's daughter ran from the corridor and I grabbed her by the arm swinging her around.

'Where is your Daddy?' I asked, but the girl stared at me wide eyed, saying nothing. 'Is he with Max?'

'I don't know what you mean,' she said, and ran away, heels kicking her bum. I looked up to the waiter.

'Excuse me…'

He turned, tray in hand, a blank stare. 'How may I help you?'

'Do you know where the others are?'

'Who?'

'The people I was with. My wife and her family. Do you know where they've gone?' The waiter frowned.

'I'm sorry sir,' he answered, 'you arrived alone.'

The shoe fits

One thing I remember clearly was that I was driving with Leila through State Forest on a winding narrow road, somewhere deep in the Southwest. It was one of those afternoons where the sun breaks through the olive foliage every so often shining the gun metal highway and applying rouge to the pebbled kerbs. I was feeling reasonably content and there seemed no reason to be unhappy. No reason at all. Soon we would be back in Albany, a log fire burning away the chilly night air. Leila would fix a meal fit for winter – perhaps some creamy pumpkin soup with fresh bread, followed by a roast dinner and apple crumble. I would have some of the red wine we had bought in Margaret River. Yes, everything would be perfect. I wanted to tell Leila how I felt but she seemed somewhat restrained, lost in her own world, so I leaned my head back against the headrest and let Vivaldi's 'Spring' complement the countryside.

'Everything will be just fine.' I murmured, looking over at Leila who had turned away from me, so I could not see her face. She was slouched deep into her seat, her arms crossed tightly and her knees pulled up in a juvenile pose. I got the distinct impression that she was upset with me and I became a little annoyed. She was spoiling a perfectly good afternoon. I wondered if I should say something, but reconsidered. After all, we would be back in Albany soon, and everything would be perfect. I would let her sulk. It was probably just a temporary thing – she was tired, that was all – and there was no need for me to become upset. If I ignored it, it would go away. Of course, it would go away. Then it occurred to me that I should make it clear that I was not going to indulge her little game of spite, so I decided to make light conversation. The cyclist struggling along the hill ahead of us seemed to afford the perfect opportunity to break the silence.

'Fancy that. Who would be cycling along this road at this hour? Probably a tourist, hey? They're the only ones mad enough to try something like that.'

'Please don't start, Edin.'

'What do you mean? I was just saying that it was odd, that's all. I mean, it's very far from the nearest town, don't you think? And the road is awfully narrow. It's not very safe, is it?'

'Here we go again…'

'What? What did I say? Honestly, Leila I'm just making an observation.'

'Nothing changes. It doesn't matter where we are, you always have to get upset over trivialities.'

'What? I'm not upset! Look…' I bit my tongue before telling her how absurdly she was behaving. It was quite unfair, but I could only make it worse by saying so. I leaned my head back again and tried to concentrate on the flowing, converging lines of the road and the music. Soon we would be home and …'

'Pull over.'

'What? Why? Honestly, Leila…'

'I need to go to the toilet.'

'Here? Can't it wait?'

'No, it can't. Leila glared at me with her dark eyes and I noticed for the first time that she had been crying. 'You say yourself that we're miles from the nearest town.' I pulled up against the kerb without saying another word and Leila got out opening the door to the crispy afternoon air.

After turning off the engine I decided to stretch my legs as well, only as soon as I walked around to the other side of the car both my feet sank deeply into the muddy clay of the verge, up to my trousers. I was cursing inaudibly, still trying to remove the dirt with ineffectual face wash towels from the dashboard, when Leila re-emerged from the bushes.

'What are you doing?'

Since it was quite obvious I decided to ignore her and carry on with the task, but with every stroke the little damp cloth merely succeeded in disintegrating while smearing the mud still deeper into my shoe.

'Honestly Edin!'

'These damn tissues are useless. Absolutely useless.' I was speaking to myself rather than to her, venting my frustration and feeling the gathering cold.

'Why did you ever take those? They're hideous! Your toes even stick out of them. You're like a child, I swear. It's as if you need someone to dress you.'

For the first time I had a good look at the shoes I was wearing and realized that I had made the trip in my bedroom slippers. My big toes did indeed protrude through the top and had been dirtied by the red clay. I couldn't even remember where I had put the shoes I had intended to wear. Quite possibly, I had left them in Margaret River. I didn't want to admit this to Leila, so I countered defensively: 'They're quite comfortable, you know. I don't really care what they look like, or whether you like them. They're comfortable and good for driving.' Leila simply shook her head but said nothing. I noticed that some of the redness in her eyes had dissipated.

'I can't possibly go in with my shoes like this.'

'You're right about that.'

'Well what do you suggest I do? I'm not getting anywhere with this,' I said, flinging one of the crumbing tissues aside. Leila shook her head again and slouched back into her seat. I had already resigned myself to not getting an answer when I heard her say:

'For heaven's sake Edin, throw them in the boot! There's a plastic sheet in there. Come on. We're already late enough thanks to you.'

This seemed quite unfair. I felt like reminding her that it had been her decision to stop the car. However when I tried to recall what we had done during the day, that part of my memory was blank. I was forced to concede that perhaps I had, unwittingly, made some error in planning. In any event it occurred to me that it would soon be academic. All would be well once we made it back to Albany, of that I was confident.

When I climbed into the car Leila appeared to be sleeping, so I started up the car and began driving. I was conscious that the light was diminishing, especially in the shadow of the forest, so I was quite eager to get out onto the major highway as quickly as possible. For one thing, kangaroos are known to come out at dusk, and I was apprehensively expecting one to hop out from behind a tree. For another, I was feeling quite tired and there was a chance I might nod off.

I was driving for what seemed an eternity, waiting for the turnoff which I could dimly recall was clearly signposted. But for mile after mile I faced the same meandering line of bitumen and the towering, silhouetted karri trees. Leila was clearly fast asleep and I contemplated waking her, then realized how foolish that would be. No, it was just a matter of time before I saw the signpost, then we would be on the home straight.

Just as I was thinking this, my headlights illuminated the white, fluorescent lettering on a sign, and my spirits lifted considerably. I strained to read the words as I approached, only I couldn't quite focus on them. My eyes were so tired that the image kept shifting and blurring. All I wanted to see was the letter 'A' – that would have been enough. However even as I brought the car to a standstill at the turnoff, no amount of neck craning and squinting helped me make out what was on the sign.

Eventually I got out, with the engine still running, and started walking over the road in my socks, but a road train coming the other way made me jump back. An endless succession of prime-movers, trucks and overloaded family vehicles followed, and I became increasingly nervous of my car with its open door standing in the middle of the intersection. I just needed to get slightly closer, that was all. Just a little closer. I wanted to shout out at the passing cars that it was unfair, that they should get the hell out of my way. Finally there was a break in the traffic, except that it was only long enough to allow me to cross over halfway. By then the night had closed in completely and since my headlights were not shining onto the sign I couldn't read anything.

The slamming of my door woke Leila who sat bolt upright. The oncoming lights glinted in her wide, confused eyes and when she spoke her voice was almost frantic.

'What's going on?'

'Nothing, nothing at all. Just go back to sleep. We'll be there soon.'

'We're not back yet? But it's night time!'

'Go back to sleep.' I tried to sound soothing but the

words came out harshly.

'We're standing in the middle of the road. There are people behind us.'

I looked in my rearview mirror and saw five or six cars banked up. One of the drivers honked his horn in annoyance. I decided to take a chance and swung the car into the darkness of the turnoff.

'The kids must be getting worried,' said Leila, almost to herself.

'The kids?'

'Yes, our children. The ones you never have time for, remember?'

Suddenly I could recall that they were waiting for us at the chalet, probably hungry because there wasn't anything in the fridge besides milk, and probably cold because neither of them was old enough to start the log fire.

'Don't worry, we'll be there soon.'

'And what were you doing back there?'

'I just wanted to check the turnoff, that's all.'

Leila snorted and sank into her seat again. Ahead of us the headlights illuminated a road that looked comparatively narrower and rougher than before. I began to doubt that I had taken the correct turn, however I didn't want to admit this to Leila and we drove the next few kilometres in silence.

A sudden bump and the sound of crunching gravel made her sit up again.

'Are you sure we're going the right way?'

I said nothing.

'The road isn't even sealed!'

'They're probably just doing road works.'

'Don't be a fool. This is just a side road.'

I ignored her and concentrated on the negotiating the progressively worsening corrugations. Fortunately we were coming up to a sealed road that intersected our path and I confidently turned left onto it, conscious that this would keep the Southern Cross directly in front of us.

'Shouldn't we turn back?'

'This will take us there. It's a main road.'

'You don't know where you're going, do you?'

'Just relax, okay. We'll get there.' As I spoke Leila shook her head and turned away again. It was clear to me that I wasn't going to enjoy the evening, no matter what happened, but then again, I no longer cared. I just wanted to get some sleep. Hopefully everything would be better in the morning.

A while later we came to a T-junction. I could tell it was a large road, probably the highway I should have been on all along, and I paused at the intersection wondering which way to turn.

'What are those police cars doing over there?' said Leila, and I followed the line of her outstretched finger to where an array of blue and red lights were flashing in the distance.

'It looks like random breath testing.'

'Maybe they can tell us the way to Albany,' said Leila, and as this seemed a sensible course of action, I pulled out and approached the flashing lights. A large arrow signalled the narrowing of the road and I could see a policeman with a reflective jacket waving me to one side with a torch.

'It's a bit strange for them to be testing way out here, don't you think,' I said. 'Maybe we're getting close to Albany.' I brought the car to a standstill as I finished speaking and I wound down the window to speak to the officer who had leaned over in preparation. Another officer had walked around to the front left-hand corner of our car where he seemed to be examining something.

'Hi there,' I said, feeling the cold air and squinting

against the torchlight which the officer briefly flung into my face. 'Can I help you?'

'Evening sir.' The name tag on his uniform read 'Amsel'. 'Do you realize that you front indicator isn't working?'

'Well no, officer. I'll see that it's fixed at the next service station. We're on our way to Albany, you see…'

'Sir, I wonder if you would get out of the car please.'

'What's all this about?' I could hear pebbles cracking like knuckles as the other officer approached.

'Please get out, sir.'

'Can you at least tell me why?' I asked, opening the door.

'We're investigating a hit and run accident sir. It involved a cyclist.' By this time I had walked around to the front of the car and the officer was staring at my socks. He looked up to his companion who, with a jerk of his head, gestured to the front corner of my car. With a gasp of horror, I saw, in the fluctuating torchlight, that it had been damaged: there was a long scratch along the bonnet and the lens of the indicator had been smashed.

'I can assure you officer, I don't know…' I stammered, looking hopefully down at Leila who seemed unaffected.

'I wonder, sir, if you could have a look at this. It was found at the scene of the accident.'

I turned to face Officer Amsel who was hidden behind his torch, and wondered what he was talking about. Then it became clear that he was referring to a parcel held by his equally silhouetted companion. A torch beam flicked up to reveal a clear plastic bag with a zip seal, smeared with reddish dirt. At first I couldn't make out what it contained – it looked like corpse of a small marsupial.

'Do you recognise this sir?' The officer handed the bag to me and I accepted it hesitantly, taking the edge of the plastic between my fingertips. Then, by the sick, yellow lamp-light, I recognized the contents only too well. I was looking at one of my bedroom slippers.

The crow

He dreams of blackness: an endless blackness, darker than the crow and more inscrutable. There is a solitary light far in the distance, a dull yellow pinpoint swallowed into the void, and he stumbles towards it on his phantom legs. The light wavers and flickers but illuminates nothing.

In the morning he sits in his chair near the window, smells the wet fragrance of autumn mixing with the musty odour of leather-covered books. The crow watches him, its head cocked to one side, one wing dragging limply on the ground. It is Sandra's bird. She thought it might learn to talk but it never has. The bird scuttles under the table as Sandra enters the room with a tray which she sets down on his lap. He stares at the steaming cup, sees the crescent shadow in the milk, the white bread spread thickly with honey and flecks of butter. When he looks up she is straightening his cardigan, her lips pursed.

'Don't worry,' she says, without looking into his eyes. 'They will go away. You'll see.' Then she is walking into the kitchen, the crow chasing her, dragging its wing. She doesn't know about the man who came into the bookstore. The man who called him by that name.

There is a knock on the door and he hears Sandra's quick, shuffling footsteps and the rustle of the blinds. The door opens a moment later and he feels the rush of cool air and street noise, a new voice.

'Guten morgen Frau Bruckner.'

'Herr Amsel! Hereinbitten.' The door jingles as it closes. 'Thank you for coming. I'm afraid I dare not leave the house.'

'Yes, I see that. They're parked over the road even now.'

'Are they? That's appalling. One of them came knocking on the door. A woman reporter with her cameraman. She was so rude. I've had to close the shop. Can you imagine? How will we live?'

'I'm afraid there's not much I can do about that Frau Bruckner. Eventually we might try for a restraining order, but for now…' His voice lowers. 'How is he taking it?'

'He's upset. I can see that. A little confused. He barely eats…'

'As difficult as it may seem, please try to leave your worries to me. After the hearing it will all be cleared up. It's a case of mistaken identity. That's all.'

'Of course it is! I've never even heard of this Doctor Gruber. It's preposterous. All they need to do is examine the photographs.'

'The difficulty is that so much time has passed. The federal police are convinced your husband and Gruber are the same man. The photographs are so old it's hard to tell anything from them.'

'Rubbish. Gruber had a lean face, didn't he? Go and have a look at Max. His face is round. It has always been round.'

'Yes, I know. The thing is, your husband's niece… she's going to testify that he is not her uncle.'

'She's lying. She doesn't know Max. She only saw him when she was a little girl. What would she know?'

'Still Frau Bruckner, I need you to help me. Can Max

tell me anything about his family? Something private that only an insider would know.'

'Max remembers nothing. Go in and see for yourself. Year after year we've waited. Nothing. After the war the Americans thought Max would be useful. He was a scientist, you know. They hoped he would recover, but he never did.' She steps out of the corridor into view. The man called Amsel looks over her shoulder, a tall figure in a dark suit. He smiles through his spectacles and Sandra speaks. 'Max, a gentleman is here to see you. He's going to help us.' Amsel bends forward, offers his right hand but quickly retracts it when he notices the cardigan sleeve pinned high on the shoulder.

He dreams of the blackness again, the same wretched light burning like a cigarette end. As he approaches its ghostly penumbra he hears the crow cawing, screaming from under his feet. He steps back to see its thrashing silhouette, one wing caught in a wire trap.

Sandra's voice startles him and he opens his eyes. It is late afternoon and the clouds have rolled in.

'If you wanted to sleep, why didn't you let me help you to bed? Come Liebchen. It's time for dinner. I'll wheel you to the television. You'd like that wouldn't you?' She pushes his chair into the lounge, presses the switch under the screen and walks away as it pops and expands from a point into loud music and credits for a finishing game show. Sandra has forgotten to switch on the lights and he sits bathed in the blue, flickering glow, the sound and smell of oil sizzling in the kitchen. On screen he sees an elderly man being wheeled along a cracked city pavement towards an intersection.

'...will face charges of war crimes, the court ruled

today…'

The camera pans up and shows Sandra's grim expression as she checks the traffic. The old man is drooling, his eyes vacant.

'…alleged to be Doctor Konrad Gruber, a leading Nazi scientist at the notorious Buchenwald concentration camp where appalling experiments were carried out on Jewish victims. He is seen here with his wife and co-accused…'

The screen fills with faces: Mr Amsel walking purposefully out of a building. He is followed by a slim, dark woman surrounded by fat, moustached detectives and microphones. She says '…my uncle died in the war. He never married.'

'Ach!' Sandra storms into the room and prods the television into silence. 'I'm sorry Liebchen.' She steps nearer and smiles crookedly, using her tea towel to wipe the moisture from his chin. For a brief moment he looks into her grey eyes, sees his silhouetted reflection against the kitchen light. Sandra bites her lip and looks away.

'Dinner will be ready soon,' she says, straightening up.

The light comes from a window, he can see that now. It escapes where the black paper has rolled back from the pane. He hears voices, familiar voices low and numbed. He hears the sound of that name. Then the screams cut through him like shards of ice and he stumbles back into the darkness. He knows what is in the room. He knows he won't remember when he wakes.

There is a loud knocking on the door, Sandra's quick shuffle. The crow skips out from under the table, bobbing its head in curiosity. Sandra is opening the door and he hears her say, 'I'm sorry the shop is closed for a while.' The response is overwhelmed by the swirl of street noise.

Moments later the door jingles as it lets the stranger in before cutting off the outside world.

'May I see him?'

'You saw him on television. That is enough.'

'I would like to make sure.' The stranger is walking into the corridor. The crow runs back to the table.

'No. Say what you have to say, then leave...' The footsteps continue and Sandra shrieks. 'I said NO!' He hears the struggle, sees the wrestling shadows. The crow peers at them with one eye.

'I MUST...' bellows the stranger as he slips out of Sandra's grasp and falls into view.

He is an old man, balding, mottled skin on his scalp, furrowed lines on his face and skinny long fingers that come up to his chin as he stares. He is the man who came in before, who called him by that name. Sandra's shadow is sitting in the corridor, sobbing.

'Is it you?' The man rolls up his sleeve and shows him the blue numbers, shadowed and diffused with age. 'Tell me... is it you Edin? It's me – Tadeuz.'

He stands in the darkness bathed in the glow from the window. The light comes from a single yellow bulb hanging from the ceiling. The only furniture in the room is a chair and he, Edin, is strapped to it. Konrad flicks at a syringe while Leila, dressed in a lab coat, looks on.

In the morning he sits in his chair near the window, smells the wet fragrance of autumn mixing with the musty odour of leather-covered books. The crow watches him, its head cocked to one side, one wing dragging limply on the ground. It is Leila's bird. She thought it might learn to talk but it never has.

Echoes of a whisper

The taxi pulled up at the kerb and I struggled to get my wallet out of my jeans pocket. After I paid the driver I stepped out into the crisp morning air, slung my backpack onto one shoulder and walked towards the hospital, which was silhouetted by the sun breaking sharply behind it. On the way I passed a man wearing a t-shirt that read: 'You can cock up your life by being a dick.'

My flight left in under an hour. Taking into account the morning traffic, I had very little time. Why was it that so many things in my life were relegated to stolen moments?

As I entered the building I was engulfed by the warmth and smell of roasted coffee beans. The cafeteria was brimming with people – exhausted night staff sipping cappuccinos, their open lab coats showing washed-out green overalls – sombre visitors sitting wordlessly opposite each other over chequered tablecloths. I walked toward the reception counter.

'Are you family?' asked the woman, her eyes cast downwards beneath a furrowed brow. When I didn't answer she regarded me blankly. 'I'm sorry sir. It says here 'family only'.' She looked down again and continued working. I stood there until I realised that I had been dismissed, then wandered uncertainly towards the door. An orderly passed by and we bumped shoulders.

'Excuse me,' he said, flashing a quick grin. I seized the

opportunity to ask him for directions. 'That would be ward forty mate,' he offered. 'Take the elevators on the south side. Don't take the ones on the north – they don't stop on that floor.' He gestured generally past the cafeteria and I thanked him, then stumbled down the corridor wondering which way was south. My eyes felt gritty and my nose was still running from the cold air. I sniffed back the clear fluid and wiped ineffectually with my sleeve wishing I had a tissue.

Before long I found a bank of elevators. One opened its stainless steel doors and spilled out a catering trolley full of clanking dishes followed by an orderly with glazed eyes. At the same time I was jostled from behind as someone rushed to get in – an angular man with olive skin and greying hair. His young daughters rushed after him. 'Let me push the button Daddy!' said the smaller one.

'No let me!'

'It's Lara's turn sweetheart. You coming in mate?' He was looking at me, holding one hand against the doors. I shook my head and smiled weakly.

I was looking for something – anything – to tell me where the elevator went, but all I could find in the sea of green wallpaper was the LED which blinked: 'G, 1, 2...' There was a long pause. '5'. I needed the fourth floor.

I was wandering along the corridor again, looking at framed black and white pictures of nursing sisters, a cabinet with old surgical instruments. I stepped aside to allow a bed to be wheeled past. The man in it had his eyes squeezed shut and jaw clenched, but the staff were chatting amiably. Then I recognised Sandra. I'd seen pictures of her on Facebook. I knew she worked at a hospital. She stopped abruptly and glared at me.

'What are you doing here?' I started to stammer in

reply, but wasn't sure what to say. I was surprised she even knew who I was. I wondered what she'd been told. 'Can't you read between the lines?' she asked. I shrugged my shoulders and she stared me down. I saw the dried snail trail my nose had left on my sleeve and I put my hands behind my back. When I looked up she was shaking her head and waving me away contemptuously. 'She's in 401. To the left as you get out of the elevator. You're lucky – her mother just left. Make it quick. The last thing anybody needs is a scene.' She walked off and I was left to look for the elevators again. I could hear her colleagues whispering as they retreated down the corridor and her saying 'I'll tell you later.'

A quick glance at my watch told me I had less than ten minutes to catch a taxi back to the airport. I'd been wandering around the hospital for almost twice that time. At that moment a side-door burst open and I caught the sight of a stairwell.

I was running up the stairs, feeling the sweat trickle under my armpits and counting the floors. When I reached the fourth I pushed open the door and fell into a stuffy warmth – the smell of baby powder and soiled nappies. I staggered down the hall, past the nursery, looking at the room numbers: 419, 418, 417… A nurse looked up from her workstation: 'Can I help you?' I forced a smile and shook my head. A happy father pushing a see-through crib nodded and winked as he passed me. I saw his baby inside, eyes wide open, a fist in his mouth and an oversize bright blue beanie covering his head.

I paused at 401, still panting. The door was closed. I took a breath and knocked gently. There was no answer. I opened it and stepped inside.

She was sitting up in bed, hunched over. Her dark hair

was matted and tangled. I couldn't tell if she even knew I was there. But when I walked over and put my hand on her shoulder, she started to sob quietly. I stood there stupidly, rubbing her bare back through the open hospital gown.

Then I heard a raspy cry, like the echo of a whisper, and I walked over to the crib near the window. He was inside, a shrivelled, writhing prune with clenched fists. I opened one of his hands with my finger and he gripped it with white knuckles. I stroked his flushed, pimpled cheeks as he flailed hopelessly from side to side, mouth gaping.

Back at the airport I sat on a moulded plastic chair in front of an LCD panel screening The Morning Show, announcements echoing over me. I saw the gate opening and people rapidly forming a queue. A man and woman embraced, then he stooped to hug his children, one of whom was crying. I picked up my backpack and hurried past them. This was, after all, just a dream. When I walked through the gate I would return to reality – to where the cobwebs of my mind would catch the memories and other detritus of time.

Flowers in the desert

I was dragged out of sleep into a frosty, hissing whiteness, my eyes so crusted and cemented I could barely open them against the glare. I felt an ache in my joints, an involuntary quivering in my body, a dryness in my mouth, nausea in the pit of my stomach. But there was no going back, so I tried to focus, struggling through the fog of a thousand confused memories – dreams, fading fast with the crystallizing present.

Isabella was there: I recognised her through the opaque blur. She came to me, floating through mist, carrying a chamois and a water bottle. I wanted to cry out but no sound came from my parched throat. Isabella did not speak: she soundlessly wiped my forehead and pressed the spout of the bottle to my mouth. The water was warm, distilled, tasteless. It flooded inside and I choked and coughed as I forgot to swallow. For a moment I savoured the warmth of her touch, her maternal presence. Then she turned away into the blurred distance and the memories rushed back with the coldness.

Out of the opacity I began to see detail: the cramped cockpit, the myriad switches, Isabella's tall, slender figure at the console. She was already dressed in fresh overalls, her dark hair tied back neatly. A slight frown of concentration creased her composure. I took another sip of the water and pushed the bottle to one side so that it drifted away and, for a moment, struggled with the wires from the monitoring pads still taped to my skin.

'Get changed. I'll need you to have a look at this.' She remained engrossed at the console. I was still searching for words – when they eventually came out, I heard my voice croaking like a rusty hinge.

'Are we there?'

'Yes.' Her long slender fingers tapped away and she continued to frown.

I got out of my chamber, with effort despite the weightlessness, pulled off my cold, sodden undergarments and grabbed fresh overalls. As I did this, I was dazzled by the brilliant albedo of the Red Planet, visible at the porthole. It took me a few seconds to squint out again and bring the ochre blur into focus.

'My God…!'

I stared through the thick glass, nausea overwhelmed, at the curving expanse below, the wispy clouds, the haloed arc of the atmosphere.

'Can this be real? Jesus!' But her back was still turned to me. 'It all pulled off! Issy…?' There was a pause before she answered.

'Not quite. We've lost contact with Houston. I've checked the transmitter and it's no longer functioning.'

'What…?' I was lifting my knees to slip into the overalls but tripped against the fabric and fell forwards.

After I was dressed I rested, watching Isabella from behind as she worked.

'That's not all.' She faced me at last. 'The back-up system's come on. We've lost all our main bank of oxygen.' She returned to the keyboard. 'It happened while we were asleep. Something hit us, probably glancing off the dish.'

I gingerly moved over to the console where Isabella

stiffened at my presence. I gave her room to move away. As she did so, I caught her glare. Clearly the months of hibernation had not erased her memory. Then she abruptly reverted to her indifferent, professional self. I turned to examine the data.

'Looks like it didn't change our course – which is damn near a miracle.'

'It did,' she said pointing to the console. 'Our trajectory was off as we were coming in. While you were asleep I had to use the thrusters to stop us from bouncing off the atmosphere.'

'How long have you been up?'

'About four hours.'

I tried to raise my voice but it faltered with the unaccustomed use.

'Why wasn't I woken at the same time?'

'Computer malfunction. Mine came on at our approach to the planet. I had to bring you out manually.'

'Christ, Issy – why didn't you wake me sooner?' Isabella stared at me unblinkingly.

'I didn't have time, Edin.' She nodded at my overalls and I realized I'd left them unzipped.

'We must have taken a pretty big knock because our velocity was way down.' She moved toward the centre of the cabin while I looked through the porthole again and saw the fringe of the polar cap, Olympus Mons projecting through the clouds, a localised dust storm raging.

'What's our status now?'

'We're in a steady orbit, pretty much as planned. There were a few tight moments though,' she said, thrusting a glucose solution at me.

'You should empty your bladder and rest for a while. You can eat something substantial later.'

'Make that much later,' I replied with a weak grin, 'I

can't even begin to think of food.' She didn't answer and I realised that the sense of bitterness was as deep as it was just prior to the launch. I wondered why we both went ahead. On my part perhaps it was an optimism that we would patch things up. On hers it seemed a calculated choice, devoid of emotion: I would not jeopardise her place in history. Whatever the reasons, the enormity of our decision and isolation hit home as I turned to face the God of War.

The surface was firmer than I expected as my feet touched it. Isabella had already descended and was opening the rover hatch, gold plating on her face shield glinting in the sharp sunlight.

'You okay?' I knew my question was redundant but felt the need to say something.

'Uh huh. Give me a hand here.'

I took a few cautious steps, still unused to the gravity despite the post-descent acclimatisation, and wary of the jagged, pock-marked rocks that littered the surface. When I looked up I saw the hatch lowering slowly to the ground and heard the hiss of the hydraulic struts. Isabella seemed to be staring into the distance.

'What do you make the temperature out there?' I said, panting a little as I approached her.

'About twenty degrees Celsius – quite warm for Mars, but then again, it is midday.' She was still staring out toward the horizon when I came alongside her. I wished I could see her face – instead my own curved image was reflected back at me.

'I don't understand,' she said, almost under her breath. 'The coordinates were quite clear. Even allowing a margin for error, we should be able to see the forward supply station.' She shifted to face me. 'Help me unload the rover and we'll head for that rise.' I watched her while she pulled the ramp into position, visualising her determined frown through the mask. Then as I bent down to straighten the wheel ramp our gloved hands touched.

'Issy, I…' She pulled away and carried on working. 'I know I can't change the past, but I want to…' She walked away from me up the ramp. 'I just want us to talk,' I finally said to her retreating back. 'That's all.' She was releasing the supports on the rover.

'There's nothing to say, Edin.'

'We can't keep on like this.'

'Like what?'

'Damn it Is, please. Give me a chance.'

Abruptly she stopped and walked out to the hatch.

'Let's get something straight: I'm here to do my job – I don't know about you. As soon as the replacement crew arrives, I'm going home. If you have something useful to say, then say it. Otherwise shut up.'

'We should be friends at least.'

The voice that came through my receiver was lowered and wavered slightly.

'I wouldn't care if you were the last person in the world – which, incidentally, you are.' She retreated from view. Moments later the rover emerged cautiously down the ramp.

We didn't speak as we progressed slowly over the larger boulders on the slope. At the zenith I held my breath momentarily, only to exhale as we were confronted with a vista of monotony. Isabella brought the rover to a halt and we sat in a baffled silence, both scanning the rock-strewn landscape. If Isabella shared my increasing sense of panic, she didn't show it. Instead she calmly got out of the vehicle, walked several metres away and raised her field glasses to her visor. I climbed out the other side.

A few minutes passed before I said: 'We've come too far. It must be further back. Maybe west of the lander.' Isabella shook her head slowly and I knew she was right. All around us the horizon yielded only the same endless boulders and a sky fading to...

'Issy!'

'What?'

'The sky. I don't know why I didn't notice before. It's blue, for God's sake!' As her helmet tipped up my image was replaced by shimmering gold. Almost directly overhead the sun appeared just a little smaller than it should, encircled by an azure heaven. My receiver blared back at me.

'And?'

'It's meant to be pink.' I looked up again to make sure. Isabella didn't not respond. When I turned back to her she was walking away purposefully.

'Did you hear what I said?' Still there was no response. I was about to call after her when I noticed an object at my feet. It was black, cord-like and partly hidden in the sand. I stooped to examine it, initially thinking it was an odd rock formation, but this impression was quickly dispelled – it looked more like a strip of dried, blackened meat. I prodded at it with my boot and it crumbled partly, like burnt newspaper. And it felt just about as light.

'Issy, come see this!' I could feel my heartbeat quickening as I straightened to see Isabella crouched next to a rock.

'No. You should come see this.'

The urgency in her voice made me run, disregarding the danger posed by the sharp, jutting terrain. My panting produced an intermittent fog in my visor and I could feel sweat trickling down my spine. Isabella was curved, hiding her discovery. She moved aside as I stumbled next to her, fine dust scattering behind.

A solitary flower was nestled in the crook of a stucco rock-face, its glassy white frond-petals cupped together into a flute, supported by a red, corded stem. The whole effect was rather like something one would expect to see at the bottom of the ocean. Only it was there, where it should not have been. We stared at it in silence. Eventually I whistled softly.

'It's alive.' Isabella turned towards me, as if for confirmation.

'It can't be.' I crouched next to her for a closer look. 'The soil on Mars is too highly oxidising...' But there was no mistake. She pointed upwards.

'What about the sky? They're the same. Neither makes any sense.' Isabella stood up and stretched her long, slender arms upwards. 'I think I've found Forward Supply anyway.' She handed me the field glasses. Her gloved finger pointed toward a distant ridge. 'Over there.' I raised the binoculars and peered through.

'Where?'

'There, on the slope, near that dry river bed. It's shiny. Can't you see?' Isabella's hand touched my shoulder while she lined up the sighting. I searched a moment longer, conscious that her hand had dropped away. Finally I saw an unmistakable metallic glint, almost hidden among the rubble.

'We need to get a move on,' she said. 'There's only enough air in these packs for another hour.' I lowered the binoculars to see that she was already walking back to the rover.

'It's strange.'

'What is?' I was at the wheel and Isabella was still looking through the glasses, even though the shiny metal was now clearly visible to the naked eye. The rover lurched as one of its drum-wheels spun briefly on a rock, then powered over.

'Well, it looks too tall, like a water tank. Wasn't the forward lander flatter?'

'Maybe it's just an optical illusion. We'll find out soon enough. Anyway, what else can it be?'

We descended onto a steep slope which marked the final run to our destination. Isabella put away the binoculars and stood up in the rover as it churned through the soft sand.

'Edin, that isn't it.'

'Come again?'

'It's some kind of building.' I could hear her breathing through my receiver: a soft panting that almost matched my own.

The 'building' grew as we approached: an aluminium sheeting that blindingly reflected the sun. I pulled up metres away. It was now clear that we had come in from behind – there was a sharp drop before the structure and a retaining wall to keep back the red sand. Even before I applied the brake, Isabella had jumped out and was walking toward the building.

'What the hell are you doing?'

'Having a look,' she said without turning around.

'Damn you, we don't know what we're dealing with.'

'The way I see it we don't have a choice. Without the forward supply, we can't last here for more than a week.'

'For God's sake, at least wait for me!' I climbed out and ran after her just as she disappeared around the front corner.

The building was basic: a cylindrical structure, aluminium walls and conical roof, plate glass windows on one side revealing an empty room. The door appeared to be made of plastic and a handle was mounted on it, somewhat higher than I expected. I cupped my hands to peer through the window. A solitary table stood at one end. Like the door it seemed to be made of plastic. A further door in the corner was closed. I looked at Isabella and saw that she was trying the handle. Then I heard the click as it opened.

As I followed Issy inside, I noticed that the floor was hard, like dry clay. A tatty, straw carpet covered it at one end. Isabella was already at the table, examining a dark earthenware bowl filled with fruit: blackened bananas, dates, withered grapes.

I heard myself saying: 'It can't be...'

Through a window on the back wall I could see into the rear 'courtyard' where another solitary desert flower was in bloom on the edge of the sand. It stared at me, quietly defiant of the corrosive sand and of logic itself.

'There's another flower...' I began, turning to Isabella, only my voice jammed when I saw that she had taken off her helmet and was combing away the strands of her dark hair. The dusty gloves left red smears on her cheeks.

'Issy!'

She looked at me blankly and said: 'It's okay.'

We stood there for several seconds, just staring at each other until Isabella's gaze suddenly averted to the window. It was a moment longer before I heard the muffled, yet growing sound of an electric engine.

The rover...?

Seconds later I saw a vehicle – a four wheeled all terrain – driving up the dry river bed. Except it immediately became clear that the river bed was in fact a road. The vehicle pulled up outside, just out of view and I heard the unmistakable sound of a handbrake, followed by footsteps. In mounting panic I lurched across the room to Isabella. Then a man stepped into the open doorway.

He was tall and slender, with pale, unblinking eyes set in a bronze face. I walked backwards towards Isabella, colliding with the table. The man gave no reaction. After a while I screamed out at him, aware that my voice was stifled in my helmet, though the receiver in Isabella's helmet blasted next to him: 'Who are you!?'

When the man answered, he spoke quickly – too quickly. The accent was strange, nasal.

'I'm Chaz – the caretaker.'

It took me a while to comprehend the words.

Eventually I said: 'We're part of Earth's Trailblazer program…'

Abruptly the man grinned and shook his head.

'Glad you could finally make it.'

'What's happening? Who are you?'

Chaz laughed, letting his head fall back. 'We've been terraforming Mars for five hundred years. Gives you an idea how long you've been missing.' He pointed to Isabella and her helmet. 'The air is good to breathe.'

I felt for the clasp on the side of my neck and pressed it. There was a hiss, a sudden pop in my ears as the air equalised. Then I lifted my helmet off, narrowing my eyes in the comparative brightness. A light breeze wafted across my face and I felt its coolness, tasted its rusty flavour. Isabella was standing by to help. I could see her so clearly now: her dark eyes, the smoothness of her skin, the dirt on her cheeks.

'How did you know…?'

Isabella paused and looked past me, through the window to the flower in the sand.

'I decided to trust,' she said quietly. Then she smiled and extended her gloved hand.

Afterword

I first published this work under the title 'A Hazy Shade of Twilight and other nightmares' in 2015. A year later, after some apparent confusion with the 'Twilight' series of books and films, I published a second edition under the present title.

This third edition, with slight restructuring, a couple of deletions and some minor editorial changes, aims to present my experiment in its final form.

Why do I call it an experiment? The project can be considered either as a collection of short stories or as a surrealist novel – it's a matter for you, the reader, to decide.

If you prefer the short story paradigm, you may consider the first fifteen chapters (which I still call 'A Hazy Shade of Twilight') as one narrative. The remaining eleven chapters would then be separate, 'nightmarish' tales.

Alternatively, you could read this project as a relatively linear science fiction narrative… that is, until the end of chapter 15 ('Dreaming') onwards, when things start to go awry. In other words, you may choose to read the project as a surrealist novel.

On one view, chapters 16 ('Shadows') to 26 ('Flowers in the desert') can be read as Edin's dreams in hibernation *en route* back to Earth from Titan.

On another view, the final chapter is actually the first and only time in the entire book that Edin is 'awake' (i.e. all the other chapters are his dreams in hibernation, albeit *en route* to Mars, not Earth).

Or maybe *everything* in this volume comprises Edin's dreams. This is especially possible in the context of my 2016 novel 'Nights of the Moon' (which can be read as a kind of 'prequel' to this project).

There are any number of interpretations. Every single one is correct.

I also leave it to the reader to decide just how much Edin's dreams reveal about him as well as the other characters. It suffices for me to say that dreams tend to contain at least some factual information.

In the case of this project, it was certainly my intention to create a single, cohesive story arc – however obliquely communicated through the device of surrealism – comprising the actions and motivations of the various characters.

Whether or not I have achieved my goal is, once again, over to you, the reader.

Dan Djurdjevic
22 January 2024

www.ingramcontent.com/pod-product-compliance
Lightning Source LLC
Chambersburg PA
CBHW061232170626
46809CB00007B/2647